Taken by Her Mates

Grace Goodwin

CHAPTER ONE

Jessica Smith, Interstellar Bride Processing Center, Earth

The dark, musky scent of my lover's skin invaded my senses as I pressed my face to the curve of his neck. I was blindfolded, but I knew him well. I didn't need my eyes to know he was mine. I knew his touch. I knew the soft glide of his golden hair beneath my fingertips and the feel of his giant cock stretching me open as he fucked me hard and fast. I knew the strength of his arms as they lifted me by my hips and settled my wet core over him, knew I would take him deep and scream his name when he finally allowed me to find my release.

I wrapped my legs around his hips and threw my head back as he filled me completely. Standing tall and strong, he was a true warrior as I knew him to be.

Up and down he lifted then released me so I slid over his hard length. Another set of hands, my second mate's gentle touch, caressed the collar around my neck. I knew the feel of his hands, knew he could be tender and gentle one moment, unbreakable and demanding the next.

I knew I pleased them well with the sight of my pussy spread open wide, my bare bottom on display. His desire

1

sparked to life within my mind through the psychic link the collar provided. But what truly drove me wild was the wet heat that built up in my core as my first mate drove deep. I squeezed him with my inner muscles, his need made apparent by the urgency of his savage thrusts.

I could sense their emotions as well as their physical desires; the connection forged by the collars we three wore was deep and completely unguarded. There was no lying, no denying lust or wants or needs. There was only truth, and love, and pleasure. So much pleasure.

"Do you accept my claim, mate? Do you give yourself to me and my second freely, or do you wish to choose another primary mate?"

The deep voice demanded an answer, sending a shiver to race over my skin and causing my pussy to clamp down on his cock with almost brutal force. He groaned with need and I bit my lip to hold in a satisfied smile. My first mate had claiming rights to my pussy until I carried his child, but my second? He had waited, patiently ensuring my body was ready to be filled by both of my mates at once.

Not willing to wait for an answer, my second mate kissed the back of my shoulder, one hand rubbing my ass, dangerously close to the dark place he would claim. His other hand wrapped around my neck in a gentle hold that made me feel helpless, weak and completely at their mercy. "Do you want us both to fuck you, love? Or not?"

My pussy clenched again and my first mate cursed, shoving me down on his cock with a single-minded intensity I had come to crave.

"Yes. I accept your claim, warriors." The formal words slipped over my lips with a sigh and I tilted my hips to rub my clit against my first mate's body even as I offered my ass to my second. "I want you both. I want you now."

The words burst from my throat, but they were not my own. I had no control over the woman whose senses I shared, I could only watch, and listen… *and feel.*

My first mate stilled beneath me and I whimpered at

being denied the fierce thrusts of his cock in my aching pussy. "I claim you in the rite of naming. You are mine and I shall kill any other warrior who dares touch you."

I didn't care who he needed to kill, I only wanted him to make me his forever.

My second mate continued to kiss his way down my spine, his next words not required by the ritual, but they were for me. Only for me.

"You are mine, mate. I shall kill any other warrior who dares *look* at you." With those words, he slowly worked a well-oiled finger into my back entrance and I cried out. Our first time would be quick, for our passions burned with too much heat to delay any longer.

I wanted them to fuck me, fill me with their seed. And then, I wanted my mates back in our quarters, naked and completely alone. I wanted to take my time with them. I wanted to rub all over their bodies, fuck and taste and explore until our scents mingled into one, until my body was too sore to enjoy any more play.

The thought brought me back to myself for a brief moment and I realized that the three lovers were not alone in the room. Male voices filled the edges of my awareness with a soft chant. I had been so focused on my mates that I had completely ignored them, until now, when their combined voices rose to fill the chamber as they spoke in unison.

"May the gods witness and protect you."

When my second mate slipped his finger from my back entrance and nudged the virgin hole with the flared tip of his cock, the others were forgotten entirely. When he pushed forward and stretched me wide... wide... wider still with two cocks filling me, I knew I was truly claimed.

"Miss Smith."

No, that wasn't either of my mates' voices. I mentally swatted it away.

"Miss Smith."

The voice came again. It was a woman's voice and one

that was stern.

"Jessica Smith!"

I startled then, my mind being pulled from the two men that surrounded me to… no, no men surrounded me. I was in the processing room. I didn't have a cock in my ass or my pussy. I didn't have two hard bodies surrounding me. I couldn't feel their heat or breathe in their potent scents. The weight of their collar was not about my neck.

I opened my eyes and blinked. Once, twice. Oh, yeah. Warden Egara. The stiff and formal woman loomed over me.

"Your testing is complete and your match has been made."

I licked my dry lips and tried to settle my racing heart. I could *feel* the men still, but it was quickly slipping away. I wanted to reach out and grab them, hang on for dear life. It was the first time I had ever felt safe and protected, cherished and desired. They weren't even my men.

I laughed dryly then and the warden raised a dark brow.

The only time I felt safe was in a dream. Reality, yeah. Reality was a bitch.

"It's over?" I asked. My voice was a little rough, as if I'd cried out in pleasure as I dreamed. God, I hoped I hadn't. It was like snoring with a new lover, but only worse. So much worse.

She must have been satisfied with whatever she saw on my face, for she nodded once and went around the simple table to sit. While she settled into a plain metal chair, I was still strapped to the processing chair, wearing just a simple hospital-style gown with the Interstellar Bride Program logo repeated across the gray fabric in a pattern. Glancing down, I could see my nipples, hard and erect, through the thin fabric. There was no question the warden saw them as well, but she said nothing.

"For the record, state your name, please."

"Jessica Smith." I squirmed in the chair, realizing that my gown was damp beneath me.

"Miss Smith, are you now, or have you ever been married?"

"No."

"Do you have any biological offspring?"

"You already know these answers."

"I do, but a verbal recording is required prior to transport. Please answer the question."

"No, I do not have any children."

She tapped her screen a few times without looking at me. "I am required to inform you, Miss Smith, that you will have thirty days to accept or reject the mate chosen for you by our matching protocols." She glanced at me. "You are the third woman from Earth to be matched to this planet. Hmm."

I had my doubts about the testing and being truly matched. I hadn't found a man on Earth who was interested in me, so it was a little depressing that I needed to search the entire universe for him.

But why then, did my testing dream have two men? What was wrong with me if I dreamed of that? Surely my mate would not be thrilled to know I had pervy dreams with more than just him.

"There will be no return to Earth if you are not satisfied. You may request a new primary mate after thirty days… on Prillon Prime. You may continue this process until you find a mate who is acceptable."

"Prillon Prime?"

I hadn't heard of it, but that didn't mean much. I hadn't heard of many of the other planets or anything about the races that inhabited them. I had been too busy with my job, with my life on Earth to even consider space. But that changed pretty fucking quickly.

"I feel like a prisoner. Is there a reason that I'm still restrained?" I flexed my wrists and bunched my hands into fists.

"Many of our volunteers, as you know, are prisoners."

"So they really aren't volunteers," I countered.

She pursed her lips. "I won't argue semantics with you, Miss Smith, but with your prior military experience you must be aware that sometimes a person is restrained for their own good. During your testing, women often become... restless. We have to ensure your safety."

"And now?" I asked.

She looked at my fists. "Now, now it is to keep you still for any preparation or body modifications that might be required prior to transfer."

"Body modifications? Warden, let me out of these restraints right now." I heard the hard edge to my voice and hoped she'd know I wasn't fucking around.

She didn't flinch. "Do not worry, you will be unconscious when they are made. You have already signed the documents and the match has been made, Miss Smith. Because of this, you are no longer a citizen of Earth, but a warrior bride of Prillon Prime, and, as such, you shall be bound by the laws and customs of your new world."

"Including being restrained?"

She cocked her head to the side. "If that is what your mate desires."

"I don't want to be matched to a man who ties me down!"

"You have been matched, Jessica, to a fierce warrior from that world. You should be proud to submit to him."

"You think just because he's a soldier that I should bow to him? What was I then? I fought. I killed."

The warden stood and came around the table.

"I know, but sometimes it is extremely difficult for women as strong as you are to find a mate dominant enough to handle your... ummm... needs."

Holy shit, was she blushing? The stiff-lipped warden was turning three shades of red. What the hell was she talking about?

"Remember, Jessica, he was matched to you as well. What you need, he will give you. It is his right, his duty and most important, his privilege." She smiled then, a wistful look in her eyes. "No more hiding. You will fight him, I can see this, but I promise he will be worth the price you will pay."

"What price?" Where the hell was she sending me? I hadn't agreed to being dominated by any man. My pussy clenched at the remembered strength of the hand around my throat in the processing simulation, but I'd yet to meet a man strong enough to take me, to bend my will. I doubted such a man existed.

"Surrender." As she spoke, the warden pressed a button near the foot of my chair and a bright blue opening appeared in the side of the wall. Still strapped securely, I could do nothing as a long, very large needle appeared and I tried to squirm, tried to fight, but I couldn't move. The needle was attached to a long metallic arm in the wall.

"Do not resist, Jessica. You are not going to be harmed. The device will simply implant your permanent NPUs."

The needle stung when it entered the side of my temple, but nothing more. Another came from the opposite wall and repeated the task on my other temple. I felt no different and so I took a deep breath. The chair lowered, much like at the dentist, but I was placed into a heated bath of some sort. Blue light surrounded me.

"When you wake, Jessica Smith, your body will have been prepared for Prillon Prime's matching customs and your mate's requirements. He will be waiting for you." She sounded rote, as if she'd said these same words over and over.

Prillon Prime. "Now?"

"Yes, right now."

Warden Egara's clipped voice was the last thing I heard above the quiet humming of electrical equipment and lights. "Your processing will begin in three... two..."

I tensed, waiting for her to finish the countdown, but a red light flashed above me and she whipped her head to the side, looking at a screen I could not see.

"No. This can't be correct." Her frown turned to a look

of shock, then confusion, all as I waited in that damn blue bathwater, naked—when had I become naked and what had happened to my gown?—and feeling like I was three-quarters drunk.

"What's happening?"

"I don't know, Jessica. This has never happened before." She scowled down at the program tablet in her hand, her fingers flying over the screen as if she were typing a very long, very complicated message.

"What is it?"

She shook her head, her eyes round and confused. "Prillon Prime rejected your transport."

What the hell did that mean? Rejected my transport? What did they want me to do, take a spaceship? Was their transport broken, or out of whatever they used to power it? "I don't understand."

"I don't either. They terminated the protocol on their end. They will not accept your arrival, or your right to claim your mate."

CHAPTER TWO

Jessica

Strapped to the table, all I could do was watch Warden Egara typing furiously on her tablet. I struggled to free myself, but knew my actions were futile. Every time the tablet would ding with an incoming message, her frown deepened, her fingers moving more quickly, with short, jerky motions, as if she wanted to punch whomever she spoke to across the vast expanse of space.

I'd learned patience the hard way in my years first in the military, then as an investigative reporter. I could stalk prey for days and never grow weary of the chase. I knew when to wait and when to shoot first. Aggression was not going to win me any points in this scenario, especially restrained, even if my frustration was so great I wanted to rip the restraints from the chair like the Incredible Hulk.

"Warden, please, tell me what's going on."

Yes, that sounded calm. Go me.

The warden bit her lip, suddenly looking every bit the young, twenty-something woman she was. Her shoulders slumped as if she carried a great weight and responsibility on her shoulders. Perhaps she did. It was her job to see all of the women—regardless of reason—well matched and safely to their destination, wherever it was in the universe. When she finally lifted her head to look directly at me, I knew by the dark cloud in her gaze that the news was not good, at least not for me.

A dark oily dread filled my gut.

"They rejected you specifically, not all Earth transport." She sighed, and I felt like I'd just been told I was the ugliest girl in first grade. Yup, the feeling was dead on. I'd felt it before, many times when *I* was the one who was denied something. Friends, lovers, jobs, family. I should have been used to it, but I wasn't. That was what made me stupid, to have hope. I hadn't realized how much I wanted to be matched to someone, someone who was just for me until I was denied. As usual.

"There is another transport occurring right now from our Bride Processing Unit in Asia, so I know it's not the system. For some reason, you are not being allowed to go. The message was sent by the Prime, *himself*."

The Prime? What the hell was a prime?

"You mean my mate?"

She shook her head absently. "No. *The* Prime. The ruler of their planet. The ruler of Prillon Prime."

His title was named after the planet itself and I was rejected by him. Great.

"Like their king?" Holy shit. Their king wasn't going to allow me to claim my mate? I'd never met this warrior mate I'd been matched to, but he was supposed to be mine and now that I was being denied, the small kernel of hope, yup, it had been hope. Shit. The *hope* I'd carried in my chest fizzled and died. It hurt.

"Yes. He is the ruler of several planets, actually, and the commander of the entire interstellar fleet," she mumbled as she looked away, unable to hold my gaze.

I cringed inwardly, nausea rising in my throat at her words. I'd been rejected by the alien king of an entire planet? Was I that bad? I was a little bossy and probably somewhat a pain in the ass. A little intense for a woman, but what woman didn't like to shoot guns and fight bad guys? Shit. The *Prime* wanted some genteel prim miss for a match to Prillon. That had to be it. Was it?

My mind in a daze, I asked the only question I could. "Why? Is it because they think I'm a drug dealer?"

I'd rather be rejected as a supposed drug dealer than a tomboy.

"Miss Smith, they don't think you're a drug dealer. They *know* you are a *convicted* drug dealer. But no, I have sent convicted murderers off-world before. I don't know why they are doing this."

She shook her head sadly and pressed a series of buttons on her tablet. I was lifted further from the water, the smooth glide distracting as I looked down at my body to discover that all my hair was gone. My head ached horribly from the new implants in my skull and my mind buzzed with noise, like static electricity crackling over a speaker.

As my body was placed back on the exam chair, Warden Egara brought a dry gray blanket to drape over me. "I'm so sorry, Jessica. This has never happened before. I will have to send a formal inquiry to the Interstellar Coalition to find out what has happened."

I was naked and dripping bluish water and I had a scratchy blanket over me, still strapped to the stupid table. How much more miserable could I get? "How long will that take?" The buzzing in my head increased.

"Several weeks, at least." Her quiet words were suddenly like a bullhorn an inch away from my eardrum and I winced.

She tilted her head when I cringed and left me for a moment, returning with an injection tube, which she pressed to the side of my neck. I flinched.

The momentary sting was worth it, as the pain in my head faded in seconds.

"I'm sorry about your discomfort. Most brides sleep through the neurostim integration process." She watched me, her eyes soft and round, kinder than at any time I'd seen

11

her. I blinked at the change, then realized what she offered wasn't concern, it was pity. I couldn't even get shipped off planet without something going wrong.

"What's a neurostim?"

"It's a neural implant that allows your mind to adopt new languages and customs. You will now be able to understand and speak any new language within a few minutes, including all the languages of Earth. This technology is only meant for those going off-planet, but since it seems you are remaining, it is quite a perk."

I blinked and tried to process what she was telling me. A perk? This was my consolation prize, the ability to speak and understand other languages? "Any language?"

She nodded once, clearly pleased with the technology, but also still confused and disappointed at my rejection. "Absolutely. Earthen or coalition."

Since I was no longer going to a coalition planet, I didn't figure that would do me much good. I had some kind of super-chip in my head that was going to allow me to understand foreign television programs or foreigners at the airport. Great. Just what I always dreamed about. I would have rather had a free car or a trip to Hawaii. Maybe some cash.

What would have been better was being transported and living out my own real-life dream, just like the processing dream where two powerful men were covering my body, fucking me like I was the most desirable woman they'd ever met, making me feel beautiful. Wanted. Loved.

No. I got the stupid in-brain translator.

I had failed my friends at the news agency, failed my friends in the police force, failed to prove my innocence in court, and now I wasn't even worthy of an alien male so desperate for a hot, wet pussy that they'd accept a mate who was a thief or murderer, without even seeing her first. Women—criminals—by the hundreds had been sent to the Interstellar Bride Program over the last few years. The women who were arrested and processed came from all walks of life. Drug addicts and traitors. Thieves and murderers.

All those women had travelled to the stars, found new homes and new lives with alien males desperate for brides through the program. Those women had been given a clean slate, a fresh start.

Me? Not me. I turned down a bribe, got framed for a crime I didn't commit, and now I'd been rejected by not just my matched mate, but the fucking king of his entire planet?

Not my best day.

"What do I do now?"

Warden Egara tilted her head and sighed. "Well, your volunteer service to the bride program was all that was required to satisfy the terms of your criminal sentence. Since no one has ever been rejected before, that is a loophole that you fall through and will most likely be rectified. I would assume in the future, a rejected woman would have to go to prison instead. For now, there are no rules regarding alternate punishment, therefore you've met all the requirements of your sentencing."

"You mean—"

"You're free to go, Miss Smith."

She lifted the edge of the blanket and wiped several drops of blue liquid from the corner of my eye where it had begun to pool and slide down my cheek like tears.

I was free. No sentencing. No prison. No off-planet hottie.

"Go home."

I didn't want to go home. I had no home. No job, no friends, and no future. Since I was supposed to be in a *galaxy far, far away*, my bank accounts had been cleared out, my home sold. When a woman went off-planet in the bride program, their belongings were divided as if they were dead. Dead and gone, never to return. I had no one to claim my toaster or my worn-out sofa, so I had to assume it was all donated to charity.

I was the first bride ever to be sent home like a dog, tail

between my legs, unworthy of an alien mate.

If I walked out the doors of the processing center and showed my face around town? Well, the creeps who set me up would send their goons to finish what they started. If they knew I was still on Earth, I'd have a price on my head within hours.

But then again, I was no pampered princess. I had a go-bag, a stash of clothing, and cash my friend in the intel business overseas had convinced me was necessary for survival. Thank God, I'd listened. All I had to do was get to my storage locker that no one knew about and I could start over. I was free. Lonely. Miserable. Hurt. But free to do whatever I wanted to do... like expose a group of corrupt officers and politicians.

The underhanded bastards thought I was gone, off-planet. No longer their problem. Perhaps that was the only luck I was going to have today.

I swung my legs off the table and smiled, suddenly filled with unexpected glee. I might not be good enough for an alien fuck, but I was very good with a telephoto lens. I thought of it as my own personal style of sniper rifle. One perfect picture was all it took to take someone down, expose their lies, ruin their life. If my camera was a weapon, then I had a hit list a half-mile long. If I was a ghost while doing it, a person who wasn't even supposed to *be* on Earth, then so much the better.

I hopped down off the table, clutching the blanket closed, but had to rethink the sudden movement when the room spun. Warden Egara's arms shot out to steady me and I nodded my thanks.

Time to go, but there was one thing the masochistic side of me needed to know. If I were to leave my off-planet opportunity here in this room, then I wanted to know. "What was his name?"

Warden Egara frowned. "Who?"

"My match?"

She hesitated, as if she were imparting state secrets, then

shrugged. "Prince Nial. The Prime's eldest son."

I laughed then, for had I left Earth, I would have been a princess indeed. Matched to an alien prince, wearing ball gowns and ridiculous shoes, my long blond hair tamed not by my normal ponytail, but with gemstone pins and elaborate twists as befit my royal station. God help me, I would have had to wear mascara and lipstick, for my pale complexion was less than beautiful when bare.

A princess? No flipping way. Perhaps that really was the reason I'd been rejected. I was absolutely, positively, *not* Cinderella.

"I think it's for the best, warden. I'm not exactly princess material." I was better with a dagger than a politician's silver tongue, more skilled with a rifle than on the dance floor. And that, sadly, was simply a fact. Whoever this Prince Nial was, he'd just dodged a bullet.

Me.

Perhaps this prince was better off without me. That didn't mean that deep down, where the emotions of that other woman's claiming ceremony lingered, the dream in which, for a few moments, I knew what it felt like to be wanted, loved, fucked and claimed by her mates, that I wasn't bleeding.

•••••••

Prince Nial of Prillon Prime, Aboard the Battleship Deston

As I lumbered to the view screen to speak to my father, I was numb. I felt as if my body weighed next to nothing, no more than a child's. It was the easiest way to handle my father if I offered no emotion.

The cyborg implants injected into my body during my time in a Hive Integration Chamber were microscopic, and impossible to remove without killing me. Hence, I was now considered contaminated, a risk to the men under my command and to the people of my planet. I was to be treated as a highly dangerous rogue. At least that was what everyone thought. Warriors who were contaminated with Hive technology were typically banished to one of the colonies to live out the rest of their lives doing hard labor. They didn't take brides. And they didn't become the Prime of Prillon's twin worlds.

My birthright, as Prime heir and prince of my people, had kept me from being immediately banished to the colonies, but there was one thing I cared about more than that and it wasn't the person who filled the screen before me.

I stared at the carefully blank face of a man twice my age. He looked quite similar to me, only older, and without any of the cyborg implants. He was huge, with a fierce face and custom armor designed to make him look even larger than his seven-foot frame. He was the Prime of two planets of hulking warriors. He had to be strong. One hint of weakness, and his enemies would take him down.

Right now, I was that weakness for him. I was the rogue son turned dangerous cyborg threat.

"Father." I bowed my head slightly in greeting, despite the rage coursing through my blood. He may have biologically been my parent, but he was no father.

"Nial, I have spoken to Commander Deston. I have filed a formal order for your transfer to the colonies."

I gritted my teeth to hold back my immediate response. So much for being numb. So, my status as blood heir to the throne was not to save me from banishment after all. He didn't give a Prillon fuck that I was his son. I was damaged, ruined by the Hive and not *worthy* of being a leader. Of being his son.

Someone handed him a tablet and he perused its content as he spoke to me, not bothering to look up. "I leave for the front in a few days to visit our warriors and assess the condition of several of our older battleships. I expect your transfer to be completed by the time I return."

I took a deep breath and tried to keep my voice as neutral

and benign as his. "I see. And what of my bride? She was due to arrive via transport three days ago."

"You had no right to request a bride. I had an agreement with Councilor Harbart. You were to claim his daughter as mate."

I couldn't help the way my hands gripped the chair in front of me.

"Harbart was a foul coward who planned to murder me and Commander Deston's bride. Why would I claim his daughter?"

The Prime raised a brow and actually looked up at me, as if confused. "The question is irrelevant now since you are... unsuitable to claim a mate. You will claim no one. Your Earth bride's transport has been denied, of course. No contaminated warrior is allowed the honor of a bride. You know this. By now, she may well be matched to another warrior who is not..."

His voice trailed off and he tilted his head, studying me. I let him look. If he were a *real* father, he'd look past the Hive's cyborg modifications and see that I was the still the same person, still his son. *Still* the prince.

"Who is not what?"

This was the first time he had seen me since my rescue from the Hive. Arms crossed, I let him take in the slight metallic shine to the skin on the left side of my face, the now odd silver coloration of the iris of my left eye, once a dark gold. I had purposely left my forearms bare so he could see the thin sheet of living biotech that had grafted to half of my arm and part of my left hand. I wanted him to see it all, yet still see *me*.

His eyes lingered on my arm. "The implants and skin grafts cannot be removed?"

Silly hope died with that one question. I'd thought *maybe* none of it would matter, but no. He only saw what the Hive had done, not his son.

"Dr. Mordin says the grafts are permanent. They'd have to take my entire arm to remove them."

"I see."

"Do you, father? What do you see?" He hadn't seen the similar Hive grafts that covered half of my left shoulder, most of my left leg, and part of my back. I could see in his cold eyes that what he had seen was plenty.

My father, the man I had never loved, but had respected and had spent my entire life trying to please, shook his head.

"I see a warrior who used to be my son." He leaned back in his chair, and the look in his eyes had gone even colder. "You will be removed from the list of heirs and reassigned to the colonies. I'm sorry, son."

"Son? *Son?* You dare call me son in the same sentence as banishing me to the colonies?" My voice had risen. Remaining calm didn't matter. It afforded me nothing.

He leaned forward to sever our connection, but my next question stopped him. "And who will be your heir?"

"You have many distant cousins, Nial. Perhaps Commander Deston will provide an heir with his new bride. If not, I'm sure the people would welcome the ancient customs once more."

The ancient customs…

"A Death Match?" He would rather see good, strong warriors fight to the death for the right to be Prime than to even consider his own son? Simply because that son had some Hive biotech grafts in his flesh?

"May the strongest warrior survive."

If I could have reached through the screen and punched him in the face, I would have. "You would see our finest warriors die?"

I'd thought the man uncaring. Unfeeling, at least toward me. I realized that it extended to everyone. He'd see strong men fight needlessly, die needlessly, all because he was… So. Fucking. Cruel.

"There is no heir. It is our way."

There hadn't been a Death Match in over two hundred years, since our ancestor had won and claimed the throne. "I am strong, father, my mind intact. There is no need to sacrifice our strongest warriors…"

I had to at least plead with the man to save the others. The strongest would rise to make a claim, and they would die, needlessly, when they should be out on the front lines, battling the Hive.

"You are contaminated."

"I have knowledge of the Hive's systems, their strategies. You would be foolish to banish me to the colonies. I should be on the front with the battle groups, where I can…"

He cut me off again. "You are no one, a contaminate. Hive. You are dead to me."

I would have argued further, but the communication cut off from his end.

Bastard. Every day for the last few years I had swung like a pendulum between the need to impress that asshole or kill him.

"I should have killed him," I murmured to myself.

I stared at the blank screen for several minutes. I'd been dismissed, and I knew I would never speak to my father again. I wasn't sorry, not anymore. Perhaps something good came from the cyborg implants. I knew where I stood with my father and he didn't deserve any more of my time or my thoughts.

No. The thought whirling in my mind in a building storm caused me far more distress. He'd refused my bride. My match. A beautiful Earth female like Commander Deston's Hannah Johnson. I had hoped for such a match, for a soft, curved female from that planet. Hannah was small, but strong and so in love with her mates, both of them, that she had begged them to take her in the claiming ceremony.

My Hive implants had given me one advantage that day, one secret I'd not shared with anyone. I had a full recording of their ceremony in my system. I watched it often in my mind, seeing again and again the way the human woman liked to be touched, the way she had arched her back, the sounds she made as her mates kissed her, touched her, fucked her. I'd wanted that for myself. Wanted a mate like that so I'd reviewed that recording until it was burned into my very soul. Learned. Memorized every bit of their ceremonial fucking.

I would make my mate scream, as they had. I would make her tremble and beg for my cock to fill her.

Witnessing the ceremony was one honor that had not been denied me by my cousin, Commander Deston. I'd watched as both he and his second, Dare, fucked Hannah like two wild men. Their human bride loved their attention, begged for more, looked at her warriors like they were the breath in her body, the very beat of her heart.

I remembered the other ceremony I'd witnessed, this one during my processing center testing. It had been the dream that had matched me to my mate. The men had been demanding, dominant, and devoted. Since my mate had been matched to me with the same dream, I knew what she would need from me. From my second.

I wanted that kind of connection that was in both ceremonies, and I would have it.

I had a match. A woman had been processed and matched to me. To that fucking hot mating ceremony. The Interstellar Bride Program's match was almost one hundred percent perfect. That left no doubt that there was a woman just for me. I had no second, no throne, and no future, but none of that mattered. The only thing—the only *person*—that mattered to me was this woman on Earth who was my mate. She'd been denied transport by my father. That didn't negate the match, the bond that we shared. It only made me want her even more. I would not be denied her. I had to wonder what she had thought of me when she'd been rejected. The hurt must have felt something like the rage I had burning inside at my father's intervention.

She would not be denied her mate, her match, just because of my asshole of a father. She would not be a victim of his machinations.

She was an innocent.

She was *mine*.

If the processing center wouldn't sanction the transport, I would simply go to Earth and take her.

CHAPTER THREE

Prince Nial, Battleship Deston, Transport Room

I walked the corridors of the battleship like a monster. Hardened warriors averted their eyes, unable to stand the sight of my silver flesh. I doubted it was because of *me*, but what could happen to them. I cared not. In a matter of hours I would be on Earth, my bride in my arms. This was a mission that would not fail.

Once my mate was secured, I would find a warrior willing to share her, I would name a second mate to protect her, and then find a way to reclaim my throne. As I walked, rage curled in a tight knot in my gut. My father was foolish, and I had spent too many years blindly following his orders. It was time to take the throne from him, by force if necessary. His tactics in the war against the Hive were ineffective and weak and I was proof of that. If not for Commander Deston's masterful leadership of the battle fleet, we would be lost already.

The transport room was nearly full. Commander Deston, his mate Hannah, and their second, Dare stood waiting for me near the edge of the transport platform. Two warriors I did not recognize worked the control station, inputting the coordinates for my transfer to Earth's processing center, where just a few days ago my mate had been turned away. Turned away! My rage only grew at how she had been rejected.

Two huge warriors stood guard at the door. At the sight of them, I realized the risk my cousin took for me. Not all on board the ship were happy to know a contaminated warrior walked among them, prince or not.

"Commander." I clasped my cousin's forearm in the old greeting, unable to express in words what this chance meant to me. By sending me to Earth to hunt my bride, he defied both my father and the entire planetary council. It showed that he had little regard for my father and a strong belief in the matching system.

I glanced at Hannah, who stood by his side. So small, so frail in comparison to her two mates, yet strong and powerful. She truly was the strong one in their bond. I glanced at their matching collars and I envied their connection.

I, too, would have that bond. Soon. I just had to get to Earth and find her and bring her home.

"Safe journey, Nial," Deston said. "Once we transport you, your father will surely lock down the transport stations and, most likely, send bounty hunters to track you down."

"I'm not afraid of my father."

Commander Deston nodded with a deep respect I'd not seen from him prior. I'd been a spoiled child before. I knew that now and I did not cower from that admission. A pampered prince who wanted to play war, but did not fully understand the costs. I was not that man any longer. I released the commander and bowed to his bride. "Lady Deston."

"Good luck." She leaned up on tiptoe and kissed me on the cheek, my left cheek. The act made me more convinced than ever that an Earth bride was my only chance of finding a female who could accept me as I was now.

Her second mate, Dare, met my gaze and I envied the

slight hint of silver in his own eye. He, too, had been captured. But as the Prime heir, I'd taken priority with the Hive, and they'd begun their work on me first. Dare had escaped their technology with only the slightest hint of silver in one eye, a hint no one but those closest to him knew about.

Dare held out his arm, and I took it. "How will you protect your mate without a second?" He held on when I would have released him. "You should choose a second, Nial. Take him with you."

"I am an outcast, a contaminate." I shook my head. "I could not ask that of any warrior. Not yet."

Still, Dare held on. "Ask what? To protect and care for a beautiful bride? To share her body and fuck her until she screams her release?" He grinned then and I saw Hannah blush. "Trust me, Nial, acting as a second mate is no hardship."

I knew the truth of his words from seeing his—their—mating ceremony in my mind.

Perhaps he spoke the truth, but I was a contaminate who was about to break Prillon law and travel to a restricted planet. I had been matched to a bride who did not know me, and would most likely run screaming at the first sight of my ruined features. I could not ask any warrior to join me under these circumstances.

Without replying, I released Dare's grip and stepped up onto the transport platform to see Lady Deston smiling at me with a mischievous glint in her unusual dark eyes. Her black hair stood out among the golden race of Prillon Prime like a star in the darkness of space. "You'll be naked when you get there, you know."

"Yes." I nodded. No clothes, no weapons. Yes, I knew Prillon's protocol, knew how our transporters were programmed to work. No clothing or weapons would pass through long range transport. Awaiting the arrival of a naked and eager bride was one of the most anticipated events in the entire Interstellar Coalition. I had to wonder what those at the processing center on Earth were going to think when a naked man—no, a naked half cyborg— appeared.

"You're also about a foot taller than most men on Earth. You're going to stick out like a sore thumb."

"I do not know what that expression means, but I have to assume that I will be a rarity just for my height alone, and not this." I pointed to the side of my face.

Hannah pursed her lips and nodded.

"So be it."

I frowned at the delay, and offered a dark glance at the warrior behind the controls to get on with it. The warrior at the controls nodded to me in acknowledgment of my unspoken command.

"Wait."

The deep voice had us all turning. One of the guards at the door stepped toward me.

His name was Ander and he'd been one of the warriors who had rescued me and Dare from the Hive. He was even larger than I, with massive shoulders and a large scar that ran the entire right side of his face. This marking was a sign of his fierceness as a warrior, the price he'd paid in the battle for our return.

My coloring was pale gold, common among our people. Ander was darker, his eyes the color of rusted steel, and his hair and skin a duskier hue, closer to brown and more common in the ancient families. Even before our rescue, I knew of him. He was greatly feared and respected on the battleship, and one of Commander Deston's elite warriors. I owed him my life. So did Dare. Having him in the transport room showed that the commander and his second both trusted him as one of their inner circle, a most faithful warrior and confidant.

I met his gaze, unflinching, one scarred outcast staring at another. I watched, curious, as he set aside his weapons and walked to face me. "I offer myself as your second."

Ander was an ugly fucker several years older than I, but

fierce in battle. I could ask for no better warrior to help me find and protect my bride. He'd proven his loyalty to me, to Dare, and to the commander over many years of battle. I did not know him well, but I knew enough. He was worthy of a bride. Hell, he was perhaps even more worthy than I.

I thought of the mating ceremony that had been the basis for the match, the one with the dominant second who had fucked his mate in the ass with expert and pleasurable precision. Knowing my mate's needs from that dream alone, I knew Ander would do. He would do quite well.

I turned to the commander, for I would not take one of his best warriors without permission. The old me, the spoiled prince who thought everything was his due, would have taken the warrior and thought nothing of that man's responsibilities to those on the ship, to those under his command, those he protected.

Ander turned to the commander as well. The commander stood with his arm around his mate's curved waist, a rare grin on his face. "Go. May the gods protect you both."

Lady Deston rested her head on his shoulder, her smile genuine. "Try not to kill too many idiots. And try not to scare her to death." She held out her hand and Dare set three black collars across her palm. She turned to me. "I think you'll need these."

I shook my head. "I regret, my lady, that they will not survive the transport. Nor will they work properly outside the ship's range."

"Oh. Then they will be here upon your return." Her hand dropped to Dare's and she gripped both of her mates, clearly upset as she studied the two of us standing shoulder to shoulder on the transport pad. "Good luck. You are going to freak her out. Try to be patient."

I nodded as I braced myself for the wrenching twist of a long range transport, Ander directly behind me. I felt the surge of power flowing through my cells that meant the transport protocol had begun. I did not understand this phrase, *freak her out.* Nor I did need to be patient. This Earth woman, she was my mate. We were matched. She would know the connection as rightly as I. She might wonder after Ander, but if I'd chosen him as my second, she did not need to question me. Her mate. There was no need to waste time courting our new bride with comely faces or kind words.

I was *her match!*

I planned to simply take her. And if my bride was afraid? If she protested the match? It would not matter. She was mine and I would not give her up. I would win her over, if it took one week or one year, she would relent.

• • • • • • •

Jessica, Earth

I crouched low on the rooftop, staring at the Drug Enforcement Agency's officers through the long lens of the camera I'd hidden in my go-bag. My target was sitting under an umbrella under one of seven tables at a private courtyard café in the heart of the city. I wore my usual recon outfit, black shirt and pants.

The officers were guests of the cartel, their presence evidence of their shady natures, proof they were on the take. Proof that I had been framed. The place was heavily guarded with goons packing heat on the ground and more men doing rooftop sweeps every hour, on the hour.

Which meant I had fifteen minutes to get the hell out of here or I'd be caught.

A woman knelt on the concrete between one man's legs, giving him a blowjob beneath the table as he sipped whiskey and joked with his friend. He didn't even pause his speech as the drugged woman took his cock down her throat and played with his balls. The entire area was filled to overflowing with drug dealers, pimps, and the prostitutes who served them, their slaves.

I wasn't sure who was worse off, the women who died

from the initial drug overdose of C-bomb or the survivors forced into slavery to get their next fix.

I hadn't eaten a full meal in two days, my body was dehydrated and my stomach filled with nothing but gel protein packs and coffee. I didn't need to survive. I had no home, no money, and no family left. Even my alien match, the one perfect man for me in all of the universe, had rejected me. All I had left was my honor, and a chance to make sure no more women were kidnapped and forced into drug and prostitution rings. This group's recruiting method, injecting captive women with a drug cocktail—called C, or C-bomb on the street, short for cunt-bomb—designed to make any woman a mindless slut. The drug worked incredibly well. After one dose, the women were either easily controlled addicts or dead.

The woman who was debasing herself with the man's cock down her throat was clearly hooked.

I watched as one of the local drug lord's lieutenants slid a bag full of drugs, money, and God only knew what else across the table to the DEA agent who opened the bag, smiled, and took a single pill—I could see the pale pink color of it through my lens—from the bag. Putting it between his thumb and first finger, he offered it to the woman sucking his cock under the table. She took it under her tongue. Almost immediately she stiffened, then smiled in a mindless haze as she lowered her head and redoubled her efforts to make him come down her throat.

With a grimace, I pressed the button and took picture after picture, careful not to move. Not yet. I needed one more name, one more face. I had already turned in three of the group's top players. A well-placed note and some photos sent to some honest cops was enough to see them behind bars. Now, I just needed to know who this group owned on the city council and I'd finish my job. I would take down the assholes who were destroying my city, or die trying.

Breathing slow and even, I didn't even twitch, not a single inch. It was hot beneath the gray tarp I used as camouflage, but I didn't dare move. The slightest reflection of the sunlight on my camera lens could alert them to my presence. I felt like a sniper, but my weapon was information, not bullets. At least not these days. When I was in the military, my M24 SWS rifle kit was much deadlier.

My patience was rewarded when a man I knew too well finally stepped from the shadows to sit down across from the two drug enforcement agents.

I blinked three times, hard, to rid my eyes of the tears gathering there. I should be surprised.

I wasn't, and that told me everything I needed to know. Every bit of my sniper training paid off in this moment. I didn't freak. I remained calm, breathed slow and even, even if my mind was moving so fast. Shit. Fuck! The fucking bastard!

Moving swiftly, I snapped several photographs before I withdrew, packed up my gear, and headed for his home. I knew exactly where it was because I'd been there before. Many times. I would set up an ambush and confront him, recording the whole thing. The city needed to know the asshole who was behind the recent string of murders, but the world would never believe me. I was a convicted criminal, one *he'd* framed. I needed a confession, and I needed it on camera.

Two hours later, he returned to his four-bedroom colonial home to find me waiting in his formal dining room on the main floor; the twelve-gauge shotgun he'd bought at a gun show years ago was loaded, the barrel resting across the high back of a cherry stained dining chair. I pointed the weapon dead center at his chest. He knew I was a damn good shot. I'd competed in shooting contests all four years in the Army, and he'd trained me himself.

"Jess." His eyes widened, completely stunned to see me. That only lasted a second before he checked his emotions.

"Clyde."

I stared at my old mentor over the top of the gun and shook my head slowly, never taking my eyes off him. He was ex-military, former chief of police, and now mayor of our great city. He sat dressed in a navy suit and tie, looking handsome and fit for his fifty years, a paragon in this city. A war hero, his eyes were framed by laugh lines. The dimple in his chin had earned him the title of the city's most eligible bachelor.

"I thought you were gone, off fucking an alien."

He had the nerve to pull a cigarette from his pocket and light it as I watched, the slow-moving smoke dancing in the stillness of the air between us.

"The alien didn't do it for you? Did you come here for a fuck, sweetheart? Another dose of C?"

"No, thank you."

He shrugged and took a deep draw on the cigarette, exhaling smoke rings as if he didn't have a care in the world. "Thought I'd offer. I hear you loved C the first time, thought you might like another go."

I shuddered. I'd told no one about that hellish night, the night I'd spent drugged out of my mind. I had locked myself in my bathroom curled in a ball on the floor. I'd masturbated until my pussy bled, thrown up over and over for hours, each orgasm only offering me momentary relief. The torture had lasted most of the night and now I knew exactly who to blame. My finger twitched on the trigger and he must have seen it, for he held his hands up in a sign of surrender.

"Easy."

"I trusted you." The thought of killing him made me want to vomit all over my boots, but I'd do it. He didn't deserve to live, but I needed a confession. Him being dead wasn't enough. My camera rested on the ledge of the fireplace, recording everything in the room, every fucking word. "Why did you do it?"

"Do what?" He stared me in the eye, calm and unhurried as he moved to sit in his favorite recliner, the one that used to have a sidearm tucked between the right arm cushion and the seat. The firearm was now safely stowed in my pocket, but he didn't know that.

"You know, set me up. Kill a few dozen innocent women. Go into business with the cartel. Sell out your city."

His hand moved to the space between the cushions and I smiled, watching his eyes change from blank to furious as he realized his weapon was gone. He sighed and lifted his hand to cross his arms across his chest.

"Do what you have to do, Jess, but you won't get a confession from me. I haven't done anything wrong."

I ached to shoot him at point-blank range, blow a hole in his chest the size of Texas, but something stopped me.

God, sometimes it sucked to have a conscience, not that this man would understand what that meant. I'd killed during my tour in the Middle East, but I'd been forced to. Kill or be killed. That was different. This? This was cold-blooded murder.

But seriously, he deserved to die.

I stared for a full half-minute, weighing my options. Kill him and run? Tie him up and call the cops?

They'd never believe me. Never. I was the sellout, the corrupt ex-military officer who'd been found with an extra million in the bank, a stash of C-bomb in my home, and the drug in my bloodstream. In this city, he was a god. I was a criminal and a liar. I was scum.

He smirked at me and the sight made me angry enough to stand and take a step forward. I was going to have to lie to him and take a chance I could push his buttons and piss him off. Force a confession. I'd left my stakeout as soon as I took his picture talking to the agents, but he didn't know what I'd seen, and what I hadn't. "I don't need a confession, Clyde. I've got you on camera at the blowjob café with a hooker between your legs and bag of drug money on the table."

"You bitch," he sneered at me, all attempts at maintaining the appearance of humanity gone. "I'm going to get you so high you won't know your own name, and then I'm going to dump you in the middle of the men.

They'll tear at you like dogs."

The neurostims in my temples buzzed and I shook my head to clear it. It happened again, louder this time, a strange noise I'd never heard before, like machines talking to each other.

I took a step back and Clyde rose from his chair, crouching to make his move while I was distracted.

Shit. Something was wrong. I lifted a hand to my temple and moaned. I had to get out of here. *Now.*

Too late. Pain shot through my temples and I dropped to my knees. The shotgun clattered to the floor as I bent over and whimpered, fighting to remain conscious.

Clyde grabbed the weapon and took one step toward me before the front door exploded inward on its hinges. Three gigantic beings stepped into Clyde's living room. They were not human. Their entire bodies were metallic, but not hard and reflective, like my grandfather's wrenches; they were soft, like metal that moved, flowing over their bodies like skin, like living tissue. Their eyes were silver but in the center, where the pupils should be, ran black dots and lines like patterns on a computer part. They had eyelids, but they did not blink as they took in the room and the man who charged them with the shotgun.

They were like something out a movie. Robots come to life. Aliens. Something definitely *not* human.

Clyde blasted one of them with the shotgun as I grabbed my camera and scrambled beneath the kitchen table, headed for the back door. My head pulsed with pain but I knew these men—or whatever the hell they were—were not here for a friendly visit. If they wanted Clyde, they could have him.

The buckshot bounced off their armor, splattering in a wide pattern throughout the room. I clenched my teeth to remain silent as I felt a piece of buckshot embed in my leg, another in my shoulder.

I'd had worse and compared to the pain in my head, it was nothing.

I was crawling out onto the back patio when I heard Clyde start screaming. Heavy footsteps moved toward me, the thud of metallic boots shaking the hardwood floor beneath my knees as one of the monsters came for me.

Giving up all pretense of stealth, I scrambled to my feet and ran, my planned escape route now coming in handy, not to flee the scene with my recording, as I'd originally intended, but to run for my life.

Clyde continued to scream in agony, but I didn't turn back. I ran, one of the creatures right behind me. It didn't matter how many times I turned, how many shortcuts I took, or places I tried to hide. He kept coming, as if I had a homing beacon…

Shit. I lifted my fingertips to the scars on the sides of each temple and cursed fate, God, and the alien prince who'd abandoned me. They did have a tracking device. It was supposed to be a fucking language translator! The crackling sound had faded, but it was still there, and I realized it was their language. True to Warden Egara's promise, as I heard more, their words became clear. Except they weren't speaking aloud, like normal people, but through some kind of broadcast frequency my new implants could pick up. It wasn't English, but I understood it perfectly.

"Find the woman. We must take her to the core."

"She is approximately seventy-two feet from our position. We will capture her in twenty-three-point-five seconds."

"The human male is dead. Get the female. We need to get off this planet before the coalition tracks our ship."

"Nineteen seconds at current position and speed."

"Increase speed."

"We will increase fifteen percent."

I briefly thought of Warden Egara and her claims regarding the implant's language mastery. She was right. If I survived this, I'd have to send her a thank-you note.

Nineteen seconds until that *thing* had me? I ran faster

than I'd ever moved in my life, thankful for once that I forced myself to work out five days a week, and ran straight into a giant chest. Stunned, I looked up, way up, saw silver flesh, and screamed.

CHAPTER FOUR

Prince Nial, Earth

The woman in my arms took one look at my face and screamed as if she had landed in the arms of the Hive hordes. She struggled, kicking and fighting my grip as relief flooded my body. I knew her face from the bride protocol files that Dr. Mordin had received prior to her transport. Prior to her *failed* transport. This was my mate, my bride. There was no doubt. Besides a visual confirmation, I *knew* she was mine. And she was terrified, but alive. And very, very beautiful.

The iron-rich scent of her blood reached me, causing rage to flood my body, battle rage like I'd never felt before. But then, I'd never before been protecting my mate. She was scared, and had been injured. I had no idea how badly. I would need to strip her of her clothing and inspect every inch of her body as soon as possible.

The thought of touching her, of exploring her curves, made my cock harden in response. I remembered the mating ceremony dream and knew instinctively what she needed, but now was not the time. Already pushed to a near frenzied state by the danger to her, I did not welcome my body's automatic response to the sweet scent of her skin and the flowery fragrance of her shining golden hair. The long strands were not dark gold, as many of my people had, but a pale color, like liquid sunlight. My personal light in the darkness. I knew only she would be able to tame the monster my cyborg implants would tempt me to become.

Speaking of monsters, the creature that pursued her would not be breathing much longer. I could hear the Hive scouts inside my mind, chattering with each other in that strange language of beeps and noise that sounded like buzzing insects inside my skull.

I had not missed that sound, but I was grateful for it now. Their noise had led Ander and me straight to them, and to my mate.

I leaned down and caught her gaze with my own, her eyes like the pale blue skies of her home world. "Jessica Smith, do not be afraid. I will not allow anything to harm you."

"How do you know my name? Are you one of them?" Her eyes wide, she stopped fighting and her gaze quickly took in the black t-shirt, pants, and leather jacket I had acquired to hide my small cache of Earth weapons. I would not need those weapons, not for the cyborg scout running toward us at full speed. I would rip him to pieces with my bare hands. In fact, I eagerly awaited his arrival.

She looked back over her shoulder, trembling, but not panicked, her small hands wrapped around my huge biceps, tugging on me in an attempt to force me to move. "It's coming in… ten seconds. Nine. Shit. We have to go."

I shook my head and gently moved her to stand behind me. "I do not run from the Hive. I will kill him for you."

Perhaps, if I could impress her with my strength and battle skills, she would allow me to claim her without the bonding influence of a Prillon mate's collar. Our bonding collars waited for us back on the commander's battleship but they would do me no good here on Earth. Until we transported back, I had only the advantage of the bonding essence in my semen to convince Jessica to accept me, but to get that to work, I had to get close enough to spread my eager cock's fluid on her flesh.

Booted footsteps pulled me from thoughts of fucking my mate and I bellowed my challenge to the Hive soldier when he rounded the corner closest to where I stood. He stopped short, staring.

I heard their chatter increase in speed and volume, but thought nothing of it as I moved forward, toward my enemy.

Behind me, my mate pressed her hands and forehead into her palms as she sank to her knees. She whimpered as if in great pain.

Their communication was hurting her somehow. I charged the cyborg, eager to rip him in half, but he turned and ran like a coward. I could not pursue him, not with my mate scared, weak, and vulnerable to attack. I knelt beside her and her fingers clutched my shirt, holding on as if I were truly her savior, her chosen mate.

Her touch, her need of me, settled deep within and I determined to earn her trust and affection. I wanted her to cling to me out of choice and desire, not fear of the Hive. I wanted her to touch me because I had become a craving in her blood, not simply a necessity to her survival. But I would accept this fragile bond between us, for now. At least she would allow me to care for her, to take her to safety and tend her wounds.

Frustrated at losing my prey, but determined to take care of my mate first, I permitted the scout's escape, filing his features away in my memory for a later hunt. He *would* die; it was simply a matter of time.

I inspected the area to be sure no threats remained before lifting my mate up into my arms. She felt perfect cradled against my chest, nothing but the thin, primitive Earthen clothing to keep the heat of her soft curves from penetrating my suddenly cool body. Lowering my face to her breasts, I breathed in the heated scent of her skin, her smell igniting a fire in my body I could barely contain. My cock hardened painfully and I growled in warning as she squirmed, kicking her legs. I pressed my lips to the curve of her breast through her soft shirt and she froze.

"What are you doing? Put me down!"

Reluctant to withdraw from the soft globes, I forced myself to lift my head. I ignored her protests and began walking to the rendezvous point Ander and I had agreed upon in a nearby park. We had positioned Warden Egara's vehicle there. Upon our arrival at the transport center, the warden had helped us locate clothing and primitive communication devices the humans referred to as cell phones. Mine was in the pocket of my jacket, where it now buzzed.

I tapped the odd device in my ear that the warden had programmed for each of us and waited for the change in sound I knew meant that the communication device had been activated.

"Speak."

Ander's voice came through clearly. "Two Hive scouts were at the human male's residence. I killed them both."

"Good. I encountered one on foot, but could not pursue."

"He will return here for the others. I will await his arrival and track him to his ship." Ander's deep voice carried clearly through the quiet air and my mate had stopped fidgeting to listen to our conversation.

"Good. Find his ship and make sure he is dead. Take his core processor. I want to know what they were doing on Earth."

"I will tear him in half, as I did the others."

I envied the smug satisfaction I heard in Ander's voice. He had experienced the supreme satisfaction of ripping a scout's body into pieces. I wanted that release, craved it. Nothing less than complete annihilation of an enemy would calm the battle rage running through my veins.

Or rutting like a wild beast in a willing female, fucking

the rage from my body with ruthless thrusts of my cock into a wet, eager pussy…

My mate wiggled, taking a quick breath and I looked down at her, thoughts of fucking replaced with surprise as she spoke. "Burn the bodies. They have to be destroyed. Their ship, too."

My eyes widened at her words.

"Why?" Destroying Hive bodies was a long, involved process. Their metal parts could take hours to melt without the proper incinerators. The ship was less of a problem. If it would not self-destruct, we would simply launch the vessel on a collision course with Earth's star where it would be incinerated instantly. If the Hive ship was nearby, we could load the dead bodies onboard and send all of them to a fiery disposal.

"So my people don't get their technology. Our scientists are smart. They can reverse engineer anything. Those *things* have to be completely destroyed."

I sighed, resigned to trust our mate's judgment. Earth was a new member of the coalition and still considered a primitive planet. They had not yet been granted full access to coalition weapons or technology. In fact, my presence on Earth violated the coalition agreement put in place to protect Earth from the Hive. Earth was off limits to all travel as coalition politicians and scientists worked with Earth's governments. Humans were not dealing well with the realization that they were one small, insignificant world among over two hundred planetary systems. Humanity was small, and still they bickered amongst themselves, undervalued their females, and had no respect for their planet.

"You are right, Jessica Smith. Humans are not to be trusted." Giving the human governments access to Hive technology would be dangerous. Humanity could not stop killing each other, despite the Hive threat. They were not ready for more power.

He pressed a spot on his shirt.

"I've opened comms so Jessica can hear you, Ander. As she said, load the bodies onto their ship and send it into their star. Leave nothing behind for their scientists."

Ander's voice came through a small speaker built in to my shirt. "Who is this female issuing orders to warriors of Prillon?"

Jessica gasped at Ander's question, but that would be nothing to the shock I knew my words would bring her.

"Our mate."

Ander's silence lasted mere seconds, but Jessica's pulse, which had begun to slow, raced once more as he addressed her directly. "Greetings, mate. I am Ander, your second; it is my duty and privilege to destroy your enemies. Then I will come to you. Your pleasure shall be the only reward I seek for tearing their heads from their bodies."

When had my second become a poet?

I looked at Jessica to judge her reaction to Ander's solemn vow. Her face was a mask of confusion.

A group of Hive killers tried to murder her. Now I held her—I didn't look any less fierce than those from the Hive—and said she was our mate. Ander was going to kill her enemies and claimed touching her body, bringing her release would be his reward. It was much to assimilate, even for a Prillon woman. But an Earth woman? I was surprised she had yet to faint.

His words had affected her, but not in the way I expected. I smelled her arousal as clearly as I smelled the blood of her wounds. The scent of her wet pussy was like a drug in my system that went straight to my hard cock. If she weren't injured, I would take her here, now. Make her mine forever.

She bit her lip, and I ached to taste her, trying, with difficulty, to focus on her words as she spoke.

"I don't understand what's going on."

Yes, as I'd expected.

She frowned, her eyebrows drawing closer to one another in an adorable shape I had seen on Lady Deston's face when she was arguing with her mates. I wanted to lean over and trace the crease between her brows with my lips, but held still as she inspected me with renewed vigor.

"You look like them. Who are you people? Why did they kill Clyde? What's the core? And why is your friend talking about being a second? What the hell is that? Then there's the vow to kill my enemies. I don't know any aliens, let alone have enemies. And his reward? I don't know who he is, why is he talking about pleasuring me and…"

Her voice trailed off as she returned her gaze to mine.

"Fucking?" I suspected she could see my need to fuck her in my eyes, for I did nothing to hide myself from her. She needed to see right away the connection we had, the almost desperate need I had for her. It was amazing really, the matching program, for I had zero doubt that she was my mate. I felt it when I saw her. It was confirmed by the feel of her in my arms. Our connection would be complete when the bonding ceremony was achieved. I didn't need a collar about my neck psychically connecting me to one about hers to know we were bonded, meant to be together. I just did, and that was truly amazing.

Gods, I wanted to bury my cock in her body and make her scream. I wanted to see her breasts quiver and shake. I wanted her absolutely mindless as I made her come over and over again. I needed her pussy to be dripping wet, my tongue buried deep, my fingers exploring her ass as I made her whimper and beg and surrender to me.

"Yes, fucking. That, too."

I had forgotten all about Ander on the other end of the conversation until her soft response made him growl with lust. Her eyes widened but Ander recovered quickly, his clipped tones clear through the earpiece.

"Take the vehicle and care for our mate. I will remove the threat and meet you at the transport facility."

He disconnected and I told my cock to stand down. My mate was in my arms, and she was bleeding. I would instruct her in her new role later after I had taken care of her wounds, when I would balance her lessons with pleasure.

Ander had been a wise choice as my second. He was fearless and powerful and I knew that his commitment to Jessica meant he would be thorough indeed in taking care of her enemies. I trusted him to eliminate both the Hive bodies and their ship. We didn't dare attempt to assume control of their vessel for the programming was too sophisticated for us to overcome and we would end up back in Hive hands.

Never again. I would die before I allowed another member of their race to touch me.

No, Ander would destroy their ship and I would take our mate to the humans' bride processing center and to Warden Egara. If my father had not yet locked down the transport relay stations in space, as I expected, I could have my mate safely back onboard Commander Deston's warship in a matter of hours.

I increased my speed to a light jog, not interested in having anyone about to see me—half man, half machine, at least to those on Earth—but the night was quiet. I passed like a shadow through a community of housing units that appeared in a long row. Cars, Earth's vehicle of choice, lined the street. Tall trees shielded the Earth's moon so only lights attached to the housing units' front entryways brightened the night.

The air was warm, close to the temperature of the climate-controlled warship, but it was damp. The air held moisture, which seemed… odd. I did not intend to remain on Earth long enough to delve into this curiosity. What I wanted to delve into was—

Jessica cried out and I glanced down at her. My pace was jostling to her, causing her pain. I stopped, prepared to take her to the ground, strip her bare, and apply field dressings to her wounds if necessary. "I smell your blood, mate."

She shook her head against my chest.

"You smell it?" she asked with surprise.

Couldn't everyone sense their mate's blood or was it just

me, due to my Hive enhancements?

"It's just a scratch. I've had worse. You can put me down now. Really, please. Thank you for your help, but you can go." Her fingers trembled and I scowled, trying to imagine the circumstances under which a female had suffered wounds so severe that bleeding through her clothing—for her shoulder was now sticky and wet with drying blood—was considered such a small thing.

"Go? Where I go, you go, mate. I can tend you now. It is my duty to ensure you are well."

She shook her head again. "No. It can wait. Just... just put me down. I need to get out of here before more of those... *things* come back."

She clung to the strange black object that hung from her neck. I knew a scope or lens of some type when I saw it, but as I had not believed the device was a weapon, I'd ignored it until now. If it were a weapon, surely she would have used it on the Hive scout chasing her. My arms tightened around her curves. I would not release her. Ever. But I understood her fear and did my best to soothe and reassure her.

"Ander will destroy them all. You do not need to be afraid. They will not come for you again."

"Them? What *are* they?"

I had tensed, expecting her to ask *What are you?* But she hadn't. Somehow, she sensed I was not any danger to her. She sensed I was her mate, her perfect match, but I doubted if she would believe it, at least not yet.

"I will explain entirely, but not here, not now."

She looked away, refusing to meet my gaze as her hands cradled the black box hanging from her neck. "I still need to go. Please, I do not need you involved in my problems. Trust me. Those things aren't the only creeps around here who want me dead."

My mate had many secrets and I was intrigued. "Creeps? They are like enemies?"

She nodded.

"If you have enemies, mate, you need but name them. I

will eliminate them immediately."

She shook her head and sighed. "You can't just go around killing people."

"Yes, I can." The confidence in my voice had her eyes widening. "Humans are small and weak. Human bones are thin, and snap like twigs." This female needed protection. She was frightened and small. Fragile. Beautiful, but weak. "It would be my great honor to destroy your *creeps* while Ander takes care of the others."

She actually smiled at me then, as if I were jesting. "That's not the point."

"Name your enemies, female. I will destroy them." Frustration replaced pride and I knew I scowled. Why would she deny me the right to protect her? Was I not worthy of this most basic gift?

She leaned back in my arms, her neck arching as she rested her head against my shoulder to look up at me. "Is this he-man thing for real? Who are you, exactly, and why do you keep calling me mate? Are you from Australia or something? Because you are a long way from home." She pushed against my shoulder. "You need to put me down. I'm not a doll."

"I am not from the continent of Australia. I am Prince Nial of Prillon Prime, your matched mate."

Her body froze, her eyes wide with an emotion I could not name. "But... but—is this a joke? Because it's not funny."

I smiled at her feisty tone, lowered my head until our lips barely touched and whispered, "You are not a child's toy, but you are mine to play with, mine to claim. You are soft and curved. Your scent makes my cock hard and my head buzz. I smell your pussy and am pleased that you grew wet and ready at your second's vow to eliminate your enemies. I, too, ask for the right to protect and care for you, just as you want and need to be cared for. You are a worthy mate. You have been matched and claimed, Jessica. The mating ceremony dream, the one where the two men dominated their mate? I can tell by the look on your face you are aware of what I speak. That is what matched us. I know what you need. Ander will help fulfill that. Together, we will pleasure you. I traveled the galaxy to come for you, mate. I will not release you. *You are mine.*"

Jessica Smith opened her mouth to argue with me, and I kissed her as I planned to fuck her, hard and fast and deep. I did not give her a chance to catch her breath. I did not want her to breathe. I wanted her to feel, to hunger, to submit.

CHAPTER FIVE

Jessica

Holy shit, the guy could kiss. It wasn't tentative. It wasn't a simple brush of his lips over mine. It wasn't quick. It was the kiss, as he said, of someone who'd traveled an entire galaxy to claim me. He'd come from Prillon Prime for me and for this kiss. Every ounce of his energy was focused on my mouth. His lips pressed into mine with the urgency of a man deprived.

Perhaps he was one, for he too had been denied his mate. The Prime's personal order had kept him from me, but also me from him. I knew he wanted me in the way his tongue plunged into my mouth and met mine. He tasted of some exotic spice, foreign and yet, absolutely heart-stoppingly familiar. I practically melted in his hold, giving myself over entirely to the kiss. To him.

I had no idea how long the kiss lasted. All I knew was my body was burning up, hotter than I'd ever been for any boyfriend—ever, and just from a kiss! Even the slight pain of my wounds only added sensation to my overloaded nerves. Remarkably, the pain woke me up, and made me want more.

Unfortunately, I wasn't going to get more. Not right now, in the middle of the street with blood running down my back and an alien prince carrying me like I was the most precious thing in the universe.

He was huge, professional football player huge. He was dressed like a clichéd bad-boy biker, all black leather and tight black t-shirt that made me want to strip it off him and run my tongue all over his massive chest and shoulders. His clothing stretched tight, like a second skin.

Never in hundred years had I assumed he was an alien, but now that I had seen his face, the slightly sharper angles, the strange metallic shimmer of the side of his face and neck, I can't believe I hadn't figured it out immediately. He was golden, his hair and one eye a dark gold, the other eye a bit lighter, like he wore a silver contact. The odd coloring of his skin disappeared beneath the collar of his shirt and I wondered if that skin felt different, and how much of his body was covered in the paler flesh. The color wasn't startling, but it was as if he'd used glitter spray and the sparkles had somehow embedded in his skin.

I wanted to taste it.

The ripped lines of his muscles made me feel small and weak and very, very feminine. That was something that at almost six feet tall myself, I was not used to feeling.

Perhaps it was his size that made me want to melt into him, but most likely my new weakness was due to the panty-melting kiss.

From the look in his eye when he lifted his head, he didn't want the kiss to end any more than I. This wasn't the place, and as he glanced around, assessing our surroundings, he knew it.

All too soon we arrived at his car and he settled me in the passenger seat of the small sedan, buckling me in and fussing as if I were a child, not a grown woman completely capable of taking care of herself. I didn't argue as his huge hands grazed my stomach and hip as he buckled me in. The heat of his touch was almost enough to push back the cold invading my limbs.

The adrenalin rush of nearly being killed by the alien things was wearing off and I knew the crash was coming on. My wounds ached, throbbing with each beat of my heart. My muscles felt weak and shaky and I had to focus to take deep, even breaths. My hands trembled and I shivered, suddenly ice cold.

He closed me in and walked around to the driver's side of the car. I choked on my laughter as he curled his large body beneath the tiny steering wheel of what was obviously a car much too small for his size. A flower-scented gel was attached to the air vents, a guardian angel pendant hung from the rear-view mirror, and the car smelled like lavender. "Whose car is this?"

"Warden Egara gave us her vehicle when we arrived." He started the engine and turned on the heater. Thank God. My teeth were actually chattering now that I didn't have his strong arms and thick heat surrounding me.

"She give you the cell phones and ear buds, too?" I wondered, leaning back against the headrest and turning to look at him.

"You are observant, bride. And yes, she gave me this primitive communication device."

He smiled and put the car in motion. We were not far from the bride processing center, if that was where he planned to take me. I didn't much care where we were going at the moment. He didn't seem to want to hurt me, which was more than I could say for most of the men walking around this city. If Clyde had known about my investigating, so did others. No one would look for me at the processing center though since no one knew I'd gone there before, so it was a good choice for a place to hide. After my previous interaction with Warden Egara, I trusted her enough to at least have a look at my wounds.

A hospital was out of the question. I'd be dead before they got my insurance information registered in their computer system. The cartel had eyes and ears everywhere.

With Clyde dead, I didn't have to worry about him telling his cartel buddies I was still here on Earth, but as soon as I showed up in the hospital's system, they'd come for me. I knew too much.

I closed my eyes and leaned my head against the doorframe, too emotionally drained to do more than close my eyes and try to figure out what the hell was going on. Clyde's death hurt, but not as much as his betrayal. That was still processing, and the ache, the feeling of lost innocence made me want to cry. He'd been like a father to me and I'd trusted him completely. Now I felt the fool, the silly little girl who looked up to her daddy with complete trust because she was too naïve, too young and green to recognize that the man holding her hand was a monster.

Clyde had been my commanding officer for two years. He'd taken me under his wing, trained me to shoot, and trained me to protect myself, encouraged me to feel invincible, to fight. He'd made me believe we were doing something good and right in the world, that we were making a difference in the fight between good and evil. And all the while, he'd been lying to me. All the while, he was the devil in disguise and I'd been blind to the truth.

As that thought filtered through my mind the pain intensified, like a knife twisting in my gut. How could he have been so evil? Why hadn't I seen it? I should have known. I should have at least suspected. Perhaps I had, and I'd simply been in denial.

Had I been so weak, so needy, that I overlooked the clues?

I'd always trusted my gut, but this time my instincts had betrayed me. That shook me more than anything else. I felt like I was on unstable ground, and I didn't like it. Not one bit.

Clyde was dead, at the hands of the Hive. I'd been rescued by my matched mate and his second, Ander. My mate! His arrival, the presence of my one perfect match in the entire universe, was more of a concern now. He was driving me about and I was completely at his mercy.

And the look of him! He was bigger than any human man I'd ever met, more defined. Just… more. He noticed my inspection and his eyes narrowed before he returned his attention to the road. "Do not worry. The Hive technology will not contaminate you."

"What?" Contaminate me? Was he crazy? Had I made the wrong call getting in the car? I could jump out when it came to a stop sign, but he'd catch me. There was no question he was bigger, stronger, more fit, and definitely sharply focused on me.

He grimaced, his hands twisting on the steering wheel until it actually looked like it might bend. "The Hive technology you see will not harm you."

"What are you talking about? The silver?"

His gaze flashed to mine as if he were surprised by my response, but I honestly had no idea what the hell he was talking about. "Yes. When I was captured by the Hive, I was tortured by their implant teams for several hours. Most of what was done to me was removed. What you see now is permanent. I also carry their mark on my shoulder, across my back, and down my leg."

I was actually beginning to feel sorry for him. The Hive had really worked him over. I'd heard too many stories about the torture and suffering of soldiers behind enemy lines. And I knew firsthand that some scars didn't show on the surface. "Is it dangerous?"

"No."

"Does it hurt?"

"No."

"Okay." I shrugged and turned my attention back to the road. "So what? Does it make you super fast or incredibly strong? Does it heal quickly or give you some kind of advantage in a fight?" I shivered, wondering what amazing things I could do with a bunch of cyborg implants. I'd be like the bionic woman times ten. I could buy a costume and do the whole superhero thing for real. That would be pretty damn cool. I'd go all black, and take down bad guys in the dark.

He remained silent so long I turned back to look at him.

"Yes. I am much stronger than most warriors. The implants also increase my reaction speed." He was watching me with a confused look on his face. "You ask odd questions. Do you not fear me?"

I choked on my laughter. I was sitting in his car, already shot and chased down by a freaky alien monster that was trying to kill me. "You're the least frightening thing I've had to deal with for days."

He frowned at me and I turned away to watch the trees pass by outside my window.

Just great. Of course I'd somehow insulted him. I'd known him for all of ten minutes, and already put my foot in my mouth. He'd rejected me before. Why was he here now? Before I'd been left stranded on that exam chair in the processing center, my transport denied, I would have felt elation and excitement, anticipation at meeting him. Now? I felt no relief. Or hope. I felt hurt. Betrayed.

Why come for me now? What had changed? Was there not someone else who was better suited? I wanted the answer, but pride prevented me asking the question. Not only was *he* here, but who the hell was this Ander? A second? What did that even mean? And why was Ander, strange alien man, so obsessed with me—I'd never even met the alien—that he was willing to kill for me and boast about it?

What bothered me even more was why the hell did that get me hot? I didn't normally go for the he-man type. Hell, I didn't date much at all. Normally, I was perfectly happy taking care of myself. In my experience men were too egotistical to deal with a strong female. They wanted whining, simpering schoolgirls who pawed all over them and told them how wonderful they were in bed, how strong and handsome and all the other constant praise that it seemed weak-minded men needed to hear.

I didn't have time for that. I was a soldier for four years. My dad was a cop, killed by a drug deal gone wrong when I was sixteen. My mom died of cancer four years later. I'd grown up without siblings or blinders on. I knew who I was and I was *not* the woman a man—or alien—traveled across the entire galaxy for. Hell, no man even drove across town for me. My parents had lived in the real world. I knew about drugs, prostitution, and corruption before my tenth birthday. Because of this, I knew how important the fight for justice truly was.

Without good people fighting for this world, it would go to hell in a handbasket. I could see the corruption, the evil tearing at the basic fabric of society. Knowing it was men like Clyde who'd only made it worse made me seethe with anger and frustration. I'd been a fighter. I'd tracked drug money, written exposé articles about corruption at every level, and I'd refused to be bought off.

My reward? I'd been set up, found guilty, and sentenced to serve a lifetime as the bride to an alien warrior I'd never met.

Until even he didn't freaking want me. Yeah, I was odd. Opinionated. Strong-willed. Too tall, too big, and too direct. I'd joined the army to learn how to fight using my body, and to college to learn to fight using my mind. I didn't play nice, I didn't lie, and I didn't take any bullshit from a man. Ever.

This guy shows up, he and his friend act like Neanderthals, swooping in to save me from the bad guys and I get horny and wet?

What the hell was wrong with me? I didn't need a man to rescue me. I didn't need a man for anything. Not even sex, not when a trusty vibrator could do the job. Except for that kiss...

"I'm losing my mind."

"You are injured and in shock. Do not worry, mate, your mind is intact."

Okay, mister hot alien. "Literal much?"

"I do not understand your question."

"Never mind. What were those things, exactly?" Turning my head again, I opened my eyes to study the man who had rescued me from certain capture. His face was strong, his features slightly more angular than a human's would be, but in no way less appealing. He filled the small space in the car like a mountain squeezed into a thimble, but he handled the vehicle with an expertise I found fascinating, as I was sure he'd never driven a car before coming to Earth.

Never mind that the sight of his strong hands conjured images of him using them to touch me, to slide those long fingers inside my body and make me come all over him. And that kiss? I wanted more. Holy hell, any conscious woman would want more. He was big and hard and made me feel things I'd never felt before, like awe. Respect. And he was part machine. From what he'd said about being captured by the Hive and used as some kind of experiment he was now, and forever would be, part machine. The idea was insane.

Even so, he was gorgeous, well-muscled, and huge, big enough to make me think he could wrestle a grizzly with his bare hands and win. The odd glistening of some of his skin acted like a beacon to my fingers. I wanted to touch it, explore him and compare the difference in his body, taste the tissue that made him stronger and faster than others of his kind. The Hive may have been trying to create a weapon they could use, but had created a formidable enemy instead.

And that made me want to crawl into his lap and stake a claim of my own. The thought of him touching another woman, carrying her in his arms, pledging to kill for her, protect her, talking of fucking her... it made me see red. I wasn't sure what I wanted from him, yet. But the thought of another woman touching him was completely unacceptable.

Besides my reaction to his sexy-as-hell appearance and size, which meant the wet heat in my panties labeled me as totally superficial, shallow, and horny, he made me feel... safe.

He made me feel protected and secure, the way my

father had before he'd been killed. Then, when he'd been gunned down I'd learned my first real truth—no one was ever safe, and no man would ever be strong enough to protect me. So I pushed down those feelings he elicited because I didn't need a man. That was my mantra. *I didn't need a man.*

Thank God Nial started talking, because while I was thinking about how much I didn't need a man, my libido was thinking about keeping him around for another one of those ridiculously hot, out-of-this world kisses. My pussy grew wet again thinking about how my lips still tingled, and I knew he could smell it. How, I had no idea, but his nostrils flared and he turned to me, his eyes burning me up in my seat, before turning back to the road.

I couldn't think about my crazy reactions to a man who was part machine. I ached for him desperately. This need, this craving, reminded me of the lust I experienced while I was high on C-bomb and I never wanted to be addicted to anything, not even a man.

Or did I? Was this how it felt to have a mate, addicted to them? Always wanting their touch, craving their attention? If so, I wasn't sure I liked it.

"The creatures you encountered were Hive scouts," he said, breaking into my thoughts. "I do not know why they were here."

I'd forgotten my question.

"The Hive?" I asked. "The alien race that forced Earth into the coalition?"

I'd read everything I could get my hands on, by any means necessary—be they legal or not—about the Hive. For the most part, the people of Earth knew what they were told. An alien race was poised to attack and the Interstellar Coalition of Planets had stepped in and offered our planet protection in exchange for soldiers and brides. The coalition didn't care where the recruits came from, only that the quota was met. The aliens didn't care that Earth's leaders chose to send convicted criminals, like me, as brides. In addition to coalition protection, Earth's leaders were well pleased to be rid of the worst dregs of society.

Since I'd been rejected by my mate, clearly the aliens had adopted higher standards these days. A thief they'd accept. A killer? No problem. But me? No. It baffled my mind and hurt deeper than any combat wound I'd ever received.

"Why would the Hive be here?" The sharp tone of my voice was partly from the lingering sting of rejection. "Even if they did all… that to you." I waved my hand in his general direction. "They haven't done anything to us here on Earth."

Earth was sending brides, and soldiers, as promised to the coalition in trade for remaining safe from the Hive. If the alien military wasn't doing their job and keeping the Hive away from us, the people of Earth needed to know about it.

I lifted the neck strap up over my head and set my precious camera, and the evidence it contained, on the floorboard between my feet. I figured I was pushing his buttons, but I didn't much care. I'd just been shot by a dear friend and chased by one of those *things*. The Hive scout—whatever that meant—had wanted me taken to something called the core. Why?

"You ask a lot of questions, mate."

"I'm not your mate," I countered. "Just answer the question."

He growled at me! Actually growled, his eyes gleaming as he lifted one hand from the steering wheel and shoved it down the front of his pants. He stroked his cock, once, twice, three times, before freeing his hand and reaching for me.

Eww! What the hell?

I scrambled to get away from his huge hand, but there was nowhere to go in the tiny car and he was huge. He grabbed my bare forearm and I felt a hint of wetness slide over my skin. *Gross!* What the hell was he doing?

I tugged, trying to resist this pervert's touch, but his grip was like a vise. A gentle one, but he wasn't going to let go. For some ridiculous reason, he was preventing me from wiping his pre-cum off my skin. For that's what it was, it had to be.

"What the hell are you doing?" I shouted.

"Sharing my essence with my mate."

"Are you crazy or just completely perverted? Yeah, the kiss was great and all, but most guys don't jerk off in front of a woman they don't know. So I'll ask again. What. The. Hell?"

Instead of answering, he grinned at me. The look he offered scared me more than anything else I'd seen that day. It was a look of absolute and total possession. "Making sure you know who you belong to."

CHAPTER SIX

Jessica

"I—"

I was poised to tell him off, because really, that was the most arrogant, domineering, bossy thing I'd ever heard, and I'd been in the military. What gave him the right to talk to me that way? What the hell gave him the right to touch me like that? He'd jerked off and—while he'd proven that he found me desirable—touched me with his pre-cum. It was gross, and creepy, and definitely perverted and—

The wet feeling on my arm changed to a buzzing heat that seemed to invade my bloodstream and go straight to my core. My nipples hardened and my pussy clenched, suddenly desperate for something to fill it. Desire raced through my body like a hit of C-bomb and I licked my lips, panting before I realized that I'd been staring at his mouth for several seconds. I ached, everywhere. For him. Only him. The tight feel of his grip, which only moments before felt restrictive and confining, now felt... secure.

Strangely, I could smell him, the scent oddly woodsy, making me want to crawl into his lap and lick him all over. I wanted his cock in my mouth. I wanted...

I glanced down at the very distinctive bulge in his pants, because I wanted it so damn bad. I clenched my core with ridiculously eager anticipation of his cock filling me.

"What the hell have you done to me? Are you trying to drug me? Using C-bomb to get a girl isn't the way to go."

His gaze raked over me before he released his hold, placing both hands back on the steering wheel.

"I don't know what C-bomb is," he replied.

"You don't know what… then why do I feel…?"

He ignored my question as we pulled into the bride processing center parking lot. The first time I'd arrived, I had entered through the volunteer entrance, in handcuffs and had not seen the front entry. It was a nondescript building and the parking lot was deserted.

The second the car rolled to a stop, I was unbuckled with my door open, ready to bolt.

I made it three shaky steps before I was lifted from the ground. "No! Put me down!"

I wriggled in his hold, but he was all hard, solid muscle. And some metal bits.

"You are injured. I will tend your wounds, mate. Then I will finish your lesson."

Lesson? What lesson? My head was screaming at me to argue with him, to force him to set me on my own two feet, but my body had other ideas. Strangely enough, the scent of his skin, so close to me, was a lure I couldn't seem to ignore. I didn't *want* to be put down and that meant what? That I'd hit my head? That I was losing so much blood that I was delirious?

That I was going insane?

My body was shaking, the three steps I'd taken revealing that I was indeed much weaker than I had suspected.

Nial carried me to the front doors of the processing center and pressed the call button on the building's exterior. We were buzzed in immediately, as if the warden had been awaiting our arrival.

As soon as the doors closed behind us I gave in to my

craving, pressing my nose to the heated skin of Nial's neck and drowning in the heat and dark musk of his body. I whimpered and closed my eyes at his heavenly scent. It was an excellent way to distract me from the pain that seemed to grow worse by the second.

I opened my eyes when I heard hurried steps. The warden came up to us wearing jeans and a blouse instead of her usual coalition uniform. Her hair was loose around her shoulders and I frowned, realizing she wasn't much older than I.

"You're very pretty."

Where had that come from? Was I drunk now, too?

She flushed, obviously pleased with my comments, her eyes darting up to Nial's face, then quickly away, as if she were uncomfortable in his presence. Maybe she was. Maybe she wanted him for herself. I couldn't blame the woman. If she felt half as… eager for him as I did, she probably wanted to climb up into his arms, too.

"Thank you, Jessica." She glanced over my body, from head to toe, but I'd been shot in the back so I knew there wouldn't be much for her to see except blood on my clothes. She looked to Nial. "Is she hurt badly?"

"Yes. I do not yet know the extent of her injuries, but while her mouth offers irritable and defiant words, she is weak and going into shock. Do you have a ReGen unit here?"

I wondered what that was, but couldn't seem to muster the strength to ask.

"No. I have a small ReGen wand, but not a complete submersion unit. Follow me." She turned on her heel and took off at a slow jog, Nial's long legs easily keeping pace as she led us to one of the exam rooms I'd seen during my processing. The warden pointed to a long exam table. "Lay her there. We will need to remove her clothing."

What? No.

Nial set me down as if I were made of porcelain. Which was sweet, until he lifted both hands to the collar of my black shirt and ripped it in half, tugging it down my arms and dropping it to the floor like it was a worthless rag.

"Hey!"

I lifted my arms to cover myself, but he wasn't looking at me as he had when I'd run into him on the street. There was no heat in his gaze now, only clinical precision.

He didn't respond to my protest but pulled off my shoes and dropped them to the floor with two loud thunks. Placing his hands on either side of my cargo pants, he ripped them in half down the crotch with seemingly zero effort, like tearing tissue paper. He pressed his hand to the center of my chest, forcing me to lie back before moving to my feet. As I pushed up onto my elbows, he deftly tugged the two halves of my pants off my body leaving me bare but for the pale pink bra and bikini panties that were covered with tiny black polka dots and trimmed with black lace. Not usual for a recon uniform, but being the only female among almost all males, lacy and frilly underthings were my sole interest in vanity. Since no man was interested in my exterior—my prickly attitude, bossiness, and tomboyish ways—the lingerie was just for me.

Nial's gaze devoured me as I lay back on the cold table so I could cross my arms over my breasts in an instinctive movement that instantly made me feel too weak, too vulnerable. This was not me. I didn't cower to any man.

Slowly, I lowered my arms and lifted my chin. I was lying on my back on the exam table and could feel the sticky wet slide of my blood under my shoulder and thigh. I stared at him until he once more lifted his gaze to meet mine, a challenge in my eyes. *Go ahead and look*, I thought. *Doesn't mean I'll let you touch me.*

"What do we have here?" Warden Egara stepped between us and I breathed a sigh of relief at being released from the intensity of Nial's gaze. I focused one hundred percent of my attention on the warden. It was much safer to completely ignore the giant alien looming over me like an overly protective, dominant alpha male, like I needed one of those in my life. I spoke to the warden.

"Twelve-gauge shotgun. My old boss was shooting the Hive scouts, but some of the buckshot must have ricocheted. I caught at least one in the shoulder, one in the thigh. If I have more, I didn't feel them." I tried to roll and found moving hurt exponentially more after every moment I remained still, as if I were becoming frozen and stiff. I winced, hissed at the pain and slumped back.

I still had the muscles that had helped me scale walls and carry heavy gear across the desert. I worked hard to keep in shape and I was grateful. If I hadn't been running faithfully since my military discharge, that Hive scout would have run me down.

"And I'm sorry about your car."

She frowned. "What about my car?"

"I bled all over the seat."

"Oh. Hush. I don't care about that."

The warden tugged on my bicep, her other hand at my hip and I tried, unsuccessfully, to stifle the moan of pain as she helped me roll onto my side. She was smaller than I by several inches and her arms and shoulders were thinner as well, more delicate and feminine.

Nial was there instantly, his large hands lifting me off the wounds and settling me so she could see where I'd been injured.

I was grumpy and bleeding, but I wasn't a total bitch. The weird reaction—the instant arousal—I'd had in the car, had faded, but with his hands on me, it returned. Just the simple placement of his palms on my skin felt hot. I savored his strength, which was odd and confusing, because I relied solely on myself. I didn't want to need anyone else's help, their strength. I needed to be strong enough on my own.

"Thanks," the warden said as she rolled a tray of medical supplies beside her. She turned to face Nial, who still held me up so she could clean and bandage my wounds. I didn't want to see what she was doing.

"This is going to hurt." Her words were the only warning

I received before a long, pointed metal object began to dig around in my flesh. Tweezers of some kind?

"Just make it fast." I winced and reached for the edge of the table. I needed something to hold onto, something to ground me in reality as she dug around in my flesh.

A warm hand completely enveloped mine, wrapping around my shaking palm and squeezing. Nial. I held on for dear life as she dug around like she was trying to tenderize a steak, not remove shrapnel.

"Don't you have something to numb it? Lidocaine or—" She stabbed deep and I sucked in air through clenched teeth. "—whiskey?"

"I can't. I'm sorry." Her voice was calm and sincere as she continued to poke and prod. "Those medications will interfere with the ReGen wand."

I had no idea what a ReGen wand was, and I didn't particularly care. But I started counting in my head, slowly, to a hundred. This wasn't my first time on the table, and this wasn't the worst wound I'd had to deal with. It hurt like a bitch, but survivable. The scars on my body were proof enough that I knew this from experience. Still, all those scars, those flaws, were one more reason I never felt comfortable naked around a man…

I opened my eyes then, curious to see Nial's reaction to the scars on my back and hip. As expected, I watched his gaze travel from one pink patch of scar tissue to the next. I expected to see curiosity, or disgust. Not rage.

"Who injured you, mate?" His gaze returned to mine, his jaw clenched. The veins in his neck and temples bulged in response to his emotions. "Tell me now, and I will kill him."

I laughed, then gasped as the warden, who had pulled the first piece of metal from my shoulder, dug in with vigor in the back of my thigh.

"You seem to want to kill a lot of things," I replied through gritted teeth.

"I would destroy entire civilizations to protect you."

Okay, whoa. He was getting a little intense for my taste.

"There's no one to kill. It was a roadside IED in Iraq."

He traced a three-inch line on my thigh with a finger and I shivered. "What is an IED, mate? I do not understand. Why did it attack you?"

I held my breath as the warden pulled the second piece of buckshot from my leg, then placed the tweezers back on the cart. Short of air, but relieved that the digging portion of today's medical procedure was over, my answer was barely more than a whisper. "It's called an Improvised Explosive Device. That—" I nodded at the line down the front of my thigh, "—was caused by a four-inch nail."

"Why were you attacked?"

I shrugged the best I could. "In a war, Nial, shit blows up. People die." Like the private who'd been standing next to me when we tripped that IED three years ago. He'd taken the brunt of the strike and died in my arms.

"Women do not fight in war."

Now I rolled my eyes. "Earth women do."

"Then it is good that I will take you off this planet. Your men are idiots."

How could I argue with that?

The warden had stepped away, but she returned with a small wand that looked like my television remote control with a glowing blue coil extending from the top. She held it above the wound in my thigh and I sighed as it felt like light was entering my body, warm and comforting and perfect. I felt no more pain there, and looked down to discover my skin, though still covered in blood, was now completely closed.

"Oh, my God. That's amazing."

She smiled and moved to my shoulder, the relief almost instant. "Do you forgive me for not injecting you with anesthetic?"

"Yes." The word was a groan as I stopped hurting. I laid my head down on the table with a deep sigh. God, that felt good.

I should have let go of Nial's hand then, but I wasn't

63

ready. Not yet. I just wanted to float for a minute and not think about the cartel, Clyde, or the Hive things hunting me. I just wanted to feel good and indulge in the warm strength of Nial's touch. Besides being free of pain, his touch felt… comforting.

But I never was good at getting what I wanted and my mind, freed of the distraction of being shot, kicked back into high gear. I had things to do. My short respite was over.

I had to get the latest batch of photos to my contacts on the police force and in the media. I had to finish what I'd started. Clyde's death would be discovered soon. I wanted to make sure the media frenzy wasn't wasted.

"I need to get my camera." I tried to sit up, but the room spun and my hand held tight to Nial's as I used him to keep from falling off the table.

"The strange black box that hung from your neck?" Nial asked.

"Yes." I tried to sit up again but a large hand settled on my chest at the base of my neck, holding me down. I lifted both hands to shove Nial's hot palm off my sensitive skin, but he didn't budge and I ended up holding onto him instead.

Frustrated, I looked up into his completely impassive face. The strength and confidence I saw in his expression made me shiver as I was forced to plead with him for permission to get up. "I left it in the car. I have to get it. It's important."

He looked down at me and the warmth was back in his gaze. Perhaps because I wasn't fighting him anymore, but clinging to him. "I will have Ander bring it inside when he arrives."

Ander. My second, whatever the hell that was. I'd forgotten about him.

"When will that be?" I shook my head and shoved at Nial's hand again. "I need it. Someone could steal it. I have to get it now."

"You will not leave the safety of this building, mate. You

need to rest for transport."

"What?" Transport? No. No. No. "I'm not going anywhere."

His eyes narrowed. "You are my mate. You will go where I command."

I choked on my laughter, and the sound wasn't happy. I could hear my hurt, my disappointment behind the fragile sound. "No, I won't. You had your chance and you rejected me. That means I'm free. My part of the bride contract was fulfilled. My obligation is over. I'm not yours anymore. You gave me up."

His eyes narrowed even further and I could see that he did not like to be denied. I could sense his anger and frustration, but did not feel a bit of it in his touch.

"I care not for your Earthen contracts, female. You are mine, my match. My father denied you transport. I had nothing to do with it and was, in fact, enraged when I discovered what he had done. Nothing has changed except that I was forced to come here to retrieve you. Let me be clear. You were not *rejected*. I will not give you up. You are mine."

I sucked in more air to argue, but Warden Egara, who'd been fidgeting uncomfortably at my bedside, held her hands up in the air. "I'll go out to the car and get the camera. No one will think a thing of it. It's my car."

Happy to ignore this very intense version of Nial, I turned to her. "Thank you."

"No problem." She turned and left the room, the large sliding door closing with a soft swooshing sound behind her.

I celebrated that small victory for about five seconds. That was when I realized I was nearly naked, and completely alone with an alien warrior who believed—very, very seriously—that I belonged to him.

CHAPTER SEVEN

Nial

My mate trembled beneath my palm, her body long and lean and so beautiful I ached to rip the small pink garments from her soft breasts and sweet pussy and taste her.

The scars on her body and in her eyes prevented me from acting on that impulse. Her own people had used her as a soldier, scarred her perfect body and taught her not to trust. My father's denial had hurt her, deeply. Now she doubted me, doubted my desire for her. It only added to the list of reasons I hated the man. No one should come between a man, his second, and their mate.

I would prove her doubts wrong, but forcing my attentions on her was not the way to win her heart. She was wounded and afraid, even under that gruff facade she maintained so well. It had dropped briefly in the car when I'd coated her skin with a hint of my pre-cum. The powers it held to bond a woman to her mates was legendary, but Prillon women did not react as my little human had. On Prillon Prime, the females would become aroused by their mates' seed, and over time, usually months, she would begin to crave intimate contact with her mates. But the bonding was slow and predictable, easy for the woman to ignore should she choose.

Not my Jessica. Her reaction had been instant and fascinating, and made me ache to fuck her, right there in the car.

Commander Deston had warned me, and I'd seen his mate's response to the bonding chemicals in his and his second's seed during their mating ceremony. I'd watched their mate writhe and beg them for more, but I had not fully comprehended the bonding power on a human female until I'd spread that small amount of pre-cum on Jessica's arm.

It hadn't taken more than three quick pumps of my cock for the fluid to seep from the tip. The moment she ran into me, I had become hard, eager for her. Ready.

Gripping her arm, letting the clear fluid seep into her skin had been an attempt to soothe her, to calm her enough that she would see reason when it came to our bond. Within a few seconds, she'd responded and the smell of her wet pussy had flooded the small interior of the car. Her pupils had dilated, and she had devoured me with her eyes, inspecting me with the gaze of a female who wanted to touch.

I wanted her hands on me more than I had ever desired anything, even the throne. She stared up at me, healed but shaken, nearly bare but not afraid, and my cock swelled even further. Gods, she was mine.

She had appeared upset by her arousal in the vehicle, but I welcomed the bond I knew my seed would help forge between us. I would wait, if necessary, slowly win over her heart and mind. Her body already recognized the truth that we were truly matched, and if seduction was the route I must take to win her over, I would be ruthless in my mastery of her pleasure.

Time and the claiming ceremony would be the answer to easing any doubts she had. Already she had melted into my arms, soft and compliant, accepting and eager for my kiss, and that had been before any of my pre-cum had touched her skin.

I would have her, my proud warrior bride.

I just needed to treat her like what she was, an aggrieved and distressed creature who feared the strong hand of a dominant mate. This was blatantly obvious to me, even in the short time I'd known her. She argued and fought, debated and cursed, but that was all an act, a fierce front to protect herself. She'd needed to build this hard exterior dealing the men of her world, but she didn't need it with me. Human men were obviously fools who had abused her trust. My arrogant father had added insult to injury.

None of that mattered as she lay weak and trembling on the table, clinging to my arm. I had to take this need she had to hold on to me as a good indication that she knew, perhaps deep within, that I was her mate, her safe place. I had to feed this gentle beginning of our bond carefully and gently.

Even though she was no longer wounded, her body completely healed, her pale eyes were round with anxiety. Her gaze darted around the room with nervous energy and she licked her lips as she stared up at me, unsure of what I would do next. The fact that she clung to me was a good sign; however, I knew she also believed herself to be untouchable right now, as she was simply waiting for the warden to return with her camera.

"Stay still, Jessica."

I took her silence as assent and was pleased as I walked to a sink on the opposite side of the room. I filled a strange bowl with warm, soapy water and grabbed a soft gray cloth from a stack of them in one of the cabinets.

The ReGen wand had healed the worst of her wounds, but I could not abide the sight of so much blood on her soft skin.

I returned to the table and dipped the towel in the water.

"I know you are overwhelmed. So much has happened to you in the past hour. It is a large adjustment. For now, you must at least sense that I mean you no harm. You are safe with me. I will let no one touch you, much less hurt you again. Will you allow me to tend to you?"

She looked at me, her eyes roving over my face, lingering on the silvery sheen of my skin, her gaze darting from my golden eye to my silver before coming to rest on my mouth. As if she realized her gaze lingered there, her focus jumped, full of guilt as her eyes met and held mine, first questioningly, then with consideration, and finally, resolve. She nodded and I helped her to sit up, the examination table covered in her blood as well.

I rolled a small, wheeled stool to the side of the table and pulled her foot forward into my lap as I began to wipe off the blood that had run down to the lower part of her leg.

My method was not perfect, but I cleaned her the best I could with slow, gentle strokes. She was allowing me to see to her, to offer her the attention and care of a mate. This wasn't sexual, but it would make the bond between us all the more powerful.

I washed her leg, then thigh. Blood had run down her back to the curve of her ass and I stood, leaning her toward me, resting her forehead on my chest so I would wash her shoulder and back. I traced the elegant line of her spine and wondered if the shiver that ran through her was the result of the water's chill as it evaporated, or if they were caused by my touch.

Warden Egara walked in with the camera just as I wrapped my mate in a new, dry blanket, lifted her into my arms, and sat down in the room's sole chair. I happily settled Jessica onto my lap. Compared to the warden, she was not a small Earth woman, but she fit perfectly. She was soft and curvy and warm and just right. She was not dainty as the warden was, and I was glad of it. I did not wish to fuck her gently and I knew that that was not what she needed. We would not have been matched otherwise.

Fortunately, Jessica continued to be compliant, which told me more than anything else how vulnerable she was feeling. Healed, yes, but still frail. The ReGen didn't return

69

spent energy. Only time and rest would resolve that, just as it would prove to her that she could trust me, that she would be safe with me. I'd seen the fire in her eyes when she'd been chased by the Hive scout and knew this quiet kitten in my arms was not her usual way.

My mate lifted her head as the warden walked in and set the camera down on the counter.

"Thank you." Her body relaxed, melting into my embrace and my cock grew hard once more as her heat molded to mine. She sighed, then spoke to the warden. "Do you have a computer I can use? I need to download the photos I took today and send them to the police."

The warden's curious gaze helped me hold my tongue as she asked what I, myself, wanted to know. "What photographs?"

With her head leaning against my shoulder, Jessica answered, "I staked out the Café Solar this afternoon."

"Oh, my God. Are you insane?" The warden, who had settled her hip against the counter, leapt to attention and Jessica tensed in my arms. A reaction I did not care for in the least.

"Probably."

I looked at the warden, not expecting an answer from my mate. "What is this Café Solar?"

She tightened her lips into a straight line, looking from Jessica to me as if trying to come to some kind of monumental decision. I used my most commanding voice. "Tell me. Now."

Jessica lifted one bare arm from within the blanket and waved the warden away, as if sparing her my ire. She was mistaken. The anger rising within was directed solely at my mate, as I suspected she had put her life in danger. Her words confirmed my suspicions.

"It's the main hangout for a drug cartel."

"*The* drug cartel. They run the entire northeast section of the country. From that restaurant." Warden Egara crossed her arms. "You *are* insane. Aren't they the ones who framed you in the first place to get rid of you? They would probably kill you on sight."

The threat to my mate rumbled through my body in a soft growl, which Jessica ignored, speaking directly to the warden.

"How do you know they framed me?" she asked. "I never told you."

The warden raised an eyebrow. "Please. I process criminals in this place every day. I know the difference between innocence and guilt and I knew your background. It wasn't hard to put two and two together."

"Thank you."

I could smell my mate's tears.

"Why are you crying? Are you in pain?" I looked down at her to find a watery smile on her face.

"No. It's just, no one else believed me."

The warden shook her head. "I wouldn't be so sure about that, Jess. But what could they do?"

"Nothing." Jessica wiped her eyes with the edge of the blanket and just that quickly, the strong, bold warrior woman was back. "Which is why I have to get those pictures downloaded and sent to the cops and my media contacts before they find Clyde's body."

The warden opened a compartment in the wall and carried a tablet to my mate. "Will this work?"

Jessica perked up quite a bit from seeing the device and flipped it onto its side, inspecting the openings there. "Yes. Thanks."

"Clyde who?" I asked.

Jessica humphed. "Clyde Tucker. The man whose house I was running from when you found me. When the Hive found me. He's also the mayor, the government leader of this city. They... the drug dealers, bought him off."

"Mayor Tucker? That asshole. I voted for him." Warden Egara's glare would have killed a Prillon warrior dead on sight. I tilted my head at her spirit, considering.

"You would make a fine mate for a Prillon warrior. You

should enter the program."

Warden Egara bit her lip and looked away until Jessica spoke to her. Jessica's voice was clipped, and she tried to pull away from my chest. I simply tightened my hold. She could do whatever she needed to do from my lap. She had no need to be jealous of my comment to the warden. I did not desire the other woman. The only mate I desired was in my arms, and I was not letting her go.

Jessica swatted at my hand where it rested on her hip but spoke to the warden. "Can you hand me my camera, please?"

"Sure."

Once Jessica had the camera, she pulled two cords from a compartment on the back of the camera I hadn't noticed before and connected them to the tablet. She asked the warden about the Internet passwords, and focused her complete attention on her task. Photographs flashed across the screen as she downloaded and categorized them, sending messages and whatever else she needed to do. I did not recognize any of the people or places in the photographs, not that I expected to. I didn't concern myself with them either, for we would not remain on Earth for long. As long as Jessica was safe, I had no issue with anyone from this planet. The only human male who had intended her harm was dead, dead at the hands of the Hive.

The Hive threat was being dealt with by my second and I was, not for the first time, grateful for Commander Deston and Dare's advice that I take a second, grateful that Ander had stepped forward. He had proven worthy, and our mate had been in more danger than either of us had anticipated.

Killing this mayor, Clyde, was the first and most likely only time that I was pleased with what the Hive had done. I just wouldn't have minded completing the task of killing the human myself. He had hurt my mate, the only thing I cared about right now.

That one thing was currently typing a message on the flat screen of the tablet the warden had given her. My Earth communication device rang and I touched the earpiece, waited for the strange blank sound of empty space.

"Speak."

"I'll be at the processing center in ten minutes. How is our mate?" Ander's arrival was good news. The sooner he arrived, the sooner we could get our mate safely off this planet.

"She was injured, but will recover. Did you find the Hive ship?"

"Yes. The last scout is dead. I sent the ship on a collision course with Earth's star."

"Did you crack their core processors?" I ran my hand up and down my beautiful mate's spine as I spoke. She had frozen in place, once more listening to my conversation with her second.

"With great pleasure."

I chuckled at that. To reach the core processor he would have had to tear their bodies in half as the special units were usually placed along the inside of the cyborg's spine, behind the heart.

"Why were they here?"

"Their orders were simple. They were after Jessica."

Shock and protective fury rose to a slow burn in my chest. "How is that possible?" I growled.

"Because she's yours. Their prime objective was to lure you into a trap so they could return you to the Hive for continued processing."

"I'll die first." Those machines would never touch me again. I would not join their Hive mind and become one with them, murder and destroy my own people.

"I think they are aware of that now. That's why they were after her."

So, the Hive leadership was more diabolical than I had envisioned. I would never surrender, forcing them to kill me rather than be taken alive again. But for the woman in my arms? My mate?

I'd barely tasted her kiss and I knew I would do anything,

sacrifice anything, to protect her. Evidently, the Hive knew it, too, and she was now a liability for me. At least that was what the Hive believed. What they didn't understand was that a Prillon mate was anything *but* a liability, and that they would simply be dealing with one Prillon warrior, but his second.

Had I come alone, the danger to her would have been twice as great. I would not take such risks with her life again. The role of a second mate was sacred and necessary. I would not second-guess the need again.

"Return here at once. She's not safe on Earth."

"Agreed. Ten minutes."

Ander disconnected and I looked to Warden Egara. She was already backing toward the door. While she had not heard Ander's response, she took one look at my expression and reached for the door handle.

"I'll go let him in."

"My thanks."

As soon as she was gone, Jessica returned her attention to her task. No more than two minutes later, she sighed and leaned across me to place the tablet and her camera back on the counter closest to us. Her Earth tasks were important to her, but were only temporary, for once we transported back to the battleship *Deston*, nothing would follow her. These small men and their crimes would be part of her past, an ugly part that would never touch her again. The closure would assist in her adjustment to her new life, knowing that she'd completed whatever was required before she left Earth behind and became completely mine.

"Are you finished, mate?" I continued to rub her back through the blanket, content that she allowed me to hold her. For now. Soon I would do much more than that. Soon I would make sure the bonding chemicals in my seed touched her once more. I enjoyed her quiet trust and acceptance of my touch, but longed to feel her fire once more. I needed to bond her to me in every way possible. I needed the connection between us to be frantic and

74

unbreakable. I needed her pussy wet and empty, aching for my cock. I needed her aching for me.

"Yes. And I hope those motherfuckers rot in prison."

I placed one hand beneath her chin and lifted her face so I could look into her eyes. So much passion and fire. I simply needed to redirect all that power and energy in my direction. The temptation to rub my seed on now was nearly too strong to resist.

"Such foul language from such a beautiful mouth." I stared at her perfectly soft, full pink lips and listened to her heart race. She licked her lips and I returned my attention to her eyes, looking into their depths, trying to figure out the mysterious combination of strength and fragility, fire and tenderness that was my mate.

"Why are you really here?" She spoke as if I were a puzzle to be solved and she couldn't quite believe the truth.

"I came for you."

"That doesn't make sense. You came here, all the way to Earth, just for me?"

"Yes."

"If that's the truth, you're insane. I'm no one, just one more piece of ass out of billions around the galaxy."

I shook my head. "You are unique and irreplaceable, the only woman in the universe matched to me." I traced her lower lip with my thumb, remembering her taste. "You felt it when my essence touched your skin. Your reaction to the bonding essence in my seed is a sign of our bond, proof of a strong connection between us. If you would rather believe in technology instead of raw animal chemistry, you can just ask Warden Egara of the success rates of the matching program. Whatever you choose to believe, know this: I am your mate and you are mine. I will always come for you. I will always protect you. I will always desire you. As will Ander, your second."

She frowned. "What second?"

"As your primary mate, it is my right and honor to choose a second warrior to love and protect you. Ander is fierce, the strongest I have seen. He alone was worthy to be your second."

"Second mate? You mean—" Her mouth fell open, her words half formed as the truth of my words hit her. She looked at me in denial. "You mean the dream sequence was accurate and—"

I tightened my hold, pulling her in closer as my thumb moved to trace the inside of her lip and explore the wet edges of her mouth. "You have two mates, Jessica. All Prillon brides are honored and gifted with two strong warriors who will care for and protect her."

"Why?"

I kissed her forehead, unable to resist tasting her. "We are warriors. We are the strongest among the member planets of the coalition. We are always on the front lines in the war with the Hive. We fight. We die. It is not our custom to leave a mate or children unprotected."

"So you, what? Take turns fucking me? I just thought that dream was just a simulation, a way to arouse me for the matching program to measure my body's responses or... something."

I kissed her temple, encouraged when she did not pull away. "No, my warrior bride." I kissed her cheek. "What you dreamed was real, although another Prillon mate and her men. It pleases me to hear that you were aroused by it, as I was."

"But—"

"We will take you together, your body filled with two hard cocks, four hands on your skin ensuring your pleasure."

"Holy shit, you're serious."

She gasped but I could smell her arousal as it filled the room. The idea of being taken by two strong warriors awakened her, as it should. We would taste her with two mouths, fill her with two cocks, worship her with four hands. There would not be a single inch of her body that was not explored, tasted, and pleasured.

The thought of rutting into her wet pussy, of planting a child in her womb as Ander took her in the ass, made me hard once more and I took the one part of her I could master here, now. Her mouth.

Holding her head exactly where I wanted it, I took her lips in a kiss as I'd wanted to since my last taste of her. I didn't tease or entice, I took what I wanted, demanding her response. My desire for her was neither shy nor gentle, it was a beast inside me raging to be set free.

I plundered her mouth, a conqueror staking my claim, the blanket forgotten as it dropped from her shoulders and bared her flesh to me. I moved one hand to cup the back of her head and tangled my fist in her hair, holding her where I needed her to be, her mouth beneath mine at the perfect angle to rule. With my free hand I explored her flesh, tracing the curve of her thigh, up her hip to the dip of her waist, up to cup the softness of her breast in the strange pink undergarment. I longed to rip it from her body, to take the hard peak of her nipple into my mouth.

She moaned softly and I continued to kiss her as I heard my second enter the room and take in the scene before him. Warden Egara's soft gasp was followed by the soft sound of her shoes in the hall as she closed the door behind her to give me exactly what I wanted as my mate shivered in my arms, unaware, lost in the pleasure I offered.

Privacy.

Ander approached softly and I opened my eyes, nodding at him slightly as I continued to take Jessica's mouth.

He was to join us, to touch our mate, to teach her what it would mean to be a Prillon bride. I'd told Jessica, as we traveled in the warden's vehicle, that I would continue her lessons and now was as good a time as any.

Ander knelt beside us, his gaze lingering on our mate's perfect feminine curves. He inhaled deeply, enjoying, as I did, the sweet scent of her wet pussy.

His face focused with intention, Ander moved to kneel between her legs as she sat sideways across my lap. I knew what he wanted, and I would help him get it.

I closed my eyes, enjoying our mate's sweet surrender as she lifted her arms and wrapped them around my neck.

CHAPTER EIGHT

Ander

Our mate was beautiful. Her golden hair fell like a silken fall of pale sunlight over Nial's arm. Her body was lean and strong, her pale skin nearly glowed next to the black of Nial's clothing, like a perfect moon in a dark sky. Her lips moved beneath Nial's with a passionate abandon that made my cock grow hard and full. She was like white fire in his arms, her full breasts covered by a small pink garment I longed to tear from her flesh. Her hands were around his neck, in full contact with the cyborg coloring of his flesh, her hand fisting with desire as a soft sound of feminine need filled the small room.

My cock was hard as a rock as I allowed my gaze to travel the long, smooth perfect of her legs to her core. I could smell her arousal, the sweetness calling to me like a siren. I had no reason to resist.

I couldn't wait to taste her pussy, to bury my tongue deep, but I knew if I moved too quickly, we could lose the power of this moment. Right now, she was soft and accepting of Nial's touch, of his kiss. I felt as if I did not touch her soon, I would explode, but I did not want to scare her. My size and appearance would do that well enough without my overly aggressive sexual needs pushing her too hard or too fast.

I was a patient man. I could stalk a target for days without eating or sleeping. I could wait a few more minutes to taste the beautiful woman who would be mine forever. *My mate.*

Her body was laid out across Nial's lap like an offering to the gods, so soft and smooth. She was not small, like Commander Deston's mate, and I was greatly relieved. She was big enough to take us both, big enough to take me.

I'd offered myself as a second mate twice before but my size and my scars had caused those warriors to fear their new mates would reject me on sight.

That I now knelt on the floor in front of my mate seemed like a dream of some kind, a fantasy that couldn't be real. That she accepted him with his cyborg flesh, kissed him with such passion, gave me hope that she could accept me as well.

Like me, Nial was damaged, scarred by the silver skin and silver eye of the cyborgs, and yet she accepted him, let him touch her. Felt desire for a warrior scarred by battle.

She was not a fantasy, but real flesh and blood. I could smell the honeyed scent of her wet core, the sweetness of her skin. I wanted to bury my tongue in her creamy heat and make her scream with pleasure. Perhaps, if I gave her pleasure before she saw my face, she would be able to see past my scars and not experience horror at the very sight of me. I was suddenly glad I had used the cleansing units aboard the cyborgs' ship before sending it on course for the center of Earth's star. I had promised our mate the death of her enemies, but now thanked the instinct that insisted I come to her without so much as a drop of blood on my hands.

She was too beautiful to be touched by such violence, too precious.

I watched Nial ply her body with pleasure, his hands

tracing her breasts, her waist and hips. He ran his hands up and down her thighs, pushing the blanket that must have been covering her lower and lower. I noticed a large scar on her thigh and wondered at the wound, but the thought fled my mind as Nial's gentle touch glided over the small piece of pink material that covered her pussy. Lingering there, he pressed his thumb to her over the fabric, rubbing her clit, then dipping into her pussy as much as the fabric would allow, then back up again to stroke her most sensitive place.

She moaned into his mouth, her hips canting to press more firmly against his touch, her lips locked to his and her tongue moving between them, exploring his mouth.

Claiming him as her own.

My head flooded with lust, with need, as my cock swelled to painful proportions. I wanted her tongue in my mouth. I wanted her to moan and writhe and scream as I brought her pleasure. I wanted her to know it was *me* touching her. Me tasting her pussy. I wanted that knowledge to make her burn.

Her reaction to Nial's touch was the signal we'd both been waiting for. He ripped the small piece of fabric from her body and she cried out in shock, her mouth torn away from Nial's kiss.

Nial took her head in both hands, preventing her from looking down her body, from seeing me, before we were ready. They locked gazes as Nial whispered his demand. I watched as her covered breasts rose and fell with her panting breaths, hard nipples outlined by the thin material. "Let us touch you."

My gaze dropped lower and as I glimpsed her wet pussy, pink and perfectly on display inches from my eager mouth. I prayed she would say yes. I couldn't wait to taste her, to suck on her clit and fuck her with my fingers and tongue. To make her come all over me.

"Nial? I can't." She licked her swollen lips. "We shouldn't be doing this. I… I don't know you and… and I…" She closed her eyes briefly. "It's… it's too much."

Her words were like a knife stabbing me in the heart, but Nial seemed unaffected.

"Shh. It will always feel like this between us. Do not fear the power of the bond between a warrior and his bride. Do not fear the pleasure we will bring you. Let go, Jessica, you are safe with me. I promise I will be here to catch you. Ander will be here to catch you. Do not be afraid to let someone else take charge. Give over and let us bring you pleasure. Let us touch you." He kissed her on the mouth, softly, with a gentleness I did not possess, and I was grateful for the divine wisdom that gave our women two males to pleasure and protect them. I could fuck her hard. I could kill for her. I could not be what Nial was. I could not be gentle or soft. I could not touch her without devouring her flesh. I needed to possess her, conquer her, own her pleasure.

I needed to make her beg.

Nial's hand glided from her neck, over her breasts, lower. Jessica's breathing became breathy pants as he moved his hand lower, over her abdomen. He stopped inches shy of her core as their eyes held. He teased her with what could be.

"Say yes, Jessica." He kissed her once. Twice. "Let go and say yes."

I saw her fingers dig into Nial's shoulders, perhaps a quick release of need or a quick burst of acceptance. She fought herself, not Nial, in her decision making. "Yes."

He rewarded her, sliding his hand down between her parted thighs and slipping two fingers deep as he took control of her mouth.

She bucked against his hand, her soft whimper of need music to my ears as he removed his fingers, now soaked with her wet juices. He held his hand up away from her body completely, making room for me to take his place.

Slowly, reverently, I touched our mate for the first time, replacing Nial's fingers with my own. Her pussy clamped down on my fingers, her hot, wet core surrounding me with welcome.

I fucked her slowly, moving my fingers in and out of her body in a smooth glide designed to bring her pleasure, but not release. I wanted her frantic for my tongue on her clit. I wanted her to beg me to taste her.

Teasing her softly, I explored her clit with my thumb as I finger fucked her, but I did not give her the pressure she wanted. She moaned in protest, lifting her hips into my touch, her mouth open, taking Nial's tongue deep as he gave her no time to think, only to feel. He held her head still, one hand buried deeply in her hair at the base of her neck. His control of her made me harder still. We would give her exactly what she needed, and she would allow it. She would submit.

Nial lowered his free hand to the front of the strange garment covering her breasts. I watched, fascinated, as a cyborg attachment emerged from the tip of his first finger, razor sharp, and cut through the fabric in less than a second, then retracted and disappeared. The garment sprang open from the center, exposing firm, full breasts with pale pink nipples. She gasped, one hand lowering from Nial's neck to try to cover herself.

Nial wrapped his hand around her wrist and lifted it back to his neck. She gave in, burying her fingers in his hair as his hand closed over one full globe, plucking and playing with her already hard nipples.

I fucked her a bit faster and explored the roof of her core, searching for the sensitive place I had read all human females had, a mythical G-spot that gave them much pleasure. Her inner walls were so slick, so hot and clenched down on my fingers when I found it…

"Oh, God."

Jessica tore her mouth from Nial's and looked down her body. She froze when she saw me kneeling there, my fingers buried to the hilt in her pussy and Nial's hand on her breast.

"Oh, my God."

She tried to close her legs, but I knelt between them, my shoulders forcing her knees to remain wide. I held her gaze as I slowly removed my fingers, sliding them deep again, brushing the spot inside her I knew would make her wild.

"Hello, mate."

I fucked her again, a little harder, watching her eyes widen as Nial took his cue from me this time. He pinched her nipple and nibbled on her ear with a little less gentleness as I fucked her with my fingers, relieved that she had no maidenhead. I did not feel like being gentle. I *could* not be gentle.

She didn't refuse me, but she didn't welcome me either, her body still tense. I slowed my pace and lowered my lips, placing a kiss over her engorged clit, flicking it with my tongue as I breathed in her womanly scent. So ripe, so hot, so perfect. I kissed one creamy thigh, then the other.

She shuddered and turned to meet Nial's gaze. "This isn't right. What are—I mean—" Jessica shook her head, even as her pussy clenched down on my fingers, demanding more than the soft kiss I'd given her. "I don't understand this. I can't feel this way with two people." She squeezed her thighs, trying to close them again. "I don't know you and... oh, God, I shouldn't be doing this."

I grinned against her pussy and laved her clit, watching for her body's every reaction. I knew she liked it, not because of the hesitancy of her words, but the way her pussy dripped all over my hand.

"Ander is your second mate. He will protect you and care for you, just as I do. Together, we will give you pleasure. This is natural and right on Prillon. You are to be cherished and pleasured by both of your mates, Jessica. It is your right as our bride." He lowered his lips to hers, tracing them with his tongue as I lowered my head and traced the edges of her clit with mine. "Do you want us to stop?"

As Nial waited for her answer, I sucked her clit into my mouth, flicking the sensitive flesh with the tip of my tongue. I sucked harder when she moaned, curving one finger to stroke her on the inside in the way I had already learned pleased her. The way she was responding, the research was well founded.

"No. Don't stop." She wrapped her legs around my head, locking me to her and I growled with approval. The vibration made her writhe and press her pussy to me, trying to force me to suck her harder and deeper into my mouth. "Don't stop."

Her demand made me ache to tie her down and teach her what it meant to try to issue orders, but I hadn't earned that right. Not yet.

First, I had to prove my worth. First, I needed to earn her trust with my fingers and my mouth. Then I would own her pleasure. Then I would make her beg.

I sucked harder, taking her to the edge over and over as I alternated finger fucking her fast and shallow, then slow and deep. Nial lowered her so her head hung over his arm and took her nipples into his mouth, one then the other, still holding her in place with his hand in her hair so she could not escape the needs we roused in her.

He shifted, moving so that he could reach for his cock with his free hand and I immediately followed suit, freeing mine from my pants and grabbing hold of it. I worked my hard length with ruthless fury as I suckled my mate's sweet essence and listened to her soft cries of pleasure. We needed our seed all over her; just the scent of it was enough to begin the connection between us, to build her desire for her mates. Having it on her skin...

We were on Earth, not on our home world where the power of the psychic bonding collars would assist us with our claim. We needed her bonded to us as much as possible, as quickly as possible. The bonding chemicals in our seed would bind her to us until we could get the mating collar around her neck.

Eager to come all over her, I worked my cock with a strong grip, but the extra force wasn't necessary. The taste of her in my mouth was enough to push me hard and fast past the point of all control.

While I kept my fingers buried deep in her pussy, I

moved to stand over her as Nial lifted his cock out of his pants and placed it on her soft stomach. I worked her clit with my thumb and watched her face as the first hard jerking motions of my cock shot a stream of thick cream onto her inner thigh, her hip, then her belly. Nial sucked her nipples into his mouth as he groaned and came all over her stomach and used his free hand to rub his essence into her creamy flesh.

Dropping my spent cock, I did the same, rubbing my warm cum into her skin, watching her body absorb it like a sponge. Intrigued, I could not tear my gaze from her face as she arched her neck, throwing her head back, her mouth open wide in a soundless scream.

Her pussy clamped down on my fingers as she came apart in Nial's arms, the bonding chemicals in our seed pushing her to her own release.

I watched her without blinking, mesmerized by the mixture of agony and bliss on her features. I knew I would never get the image of her pleasure out of my mind. I would never forget this perfect moment.

I dropped to my knees and sucked her clit into my mouth once again, drawing out her pleasure as she came, her soft screams fading to whimpers as we acted like the greedy Prillon mates I knew us to be and used our hands and our mouths to push her over the edge again and again. We took and took until she had nothing left to give, until she lay limp with complete exhaustion. Only then did Nial wrap the blanket about her and stand. I wiped her salty, tangy essence from my lips and chin as I, too, rose to follow Nial as he carried our mate to the transport chamber.

There, Warden Egara waited for us. She blushed slightly at our entry, but busied herself with the instrumentation before her.

"Send us back to Commander Deston's battleship," Nial commanded.

"I'm sorry. I can't," she replied. "The Prime has shut down all transport beyond the second zone."

I shook my head and looked at Nial, who carried our naked, sleepy mate. Jessica's head was tucked securely beneath his chin and she was completely relaxed in his arms, trusting us to take care of her. My heart swelled with pride knowing I'd helped put that contented, submissive languor in her bones. She was no longer pale, a flush of arousal lingered on her cheeks and her gaze drifted about without care or concern, safe as she was with her mates surrounding her.

"That means the only planet my father left within transport range of Earth is the Colony."

I recognized the rage in Nial's voice. I felt it myself. The Prime had made it impossible for us to take our mate home. Taking her to the Colony would be dangerous. The entire planet was populated with contaminated warriors, those who had been taken by the Hive and *altered*, as Nial had been. The men there were all outcasts, captured, tortured, and then rejected by their own people, abandoned to live out their days alone and without mates on another world.

I looked at our mate, at her beautiful face and soft curves and knew she would most likely be the only female on the entire planet. I knew, even before Nial spoke, what he would choose. As Jessica's primary mate, he carried full authority in this situation.

"We have no choice, Ander. The Hive hunt for her. We cannot remain on Earth. It's not safe for our mate." Nial looked at me and I nodded, rolling my shoulders in preparation for battle. Just in case.

"The colony may be no better than this place." We were taking our mate into unfamiliar territory with no weapons but our own fists. If the warriors who had been banished to the colony were angry or vengeful, or unfriendly to outsiders, we could regret the decision to take our mate amongst them.

"If we must, we can steal a transport ship and travel to the battleship *Deston* from there." He looked down at Jessica, who appeared to be asleep in his arms. "If we stay here, the danger to our mate is tenfold. The Hive will send additional scouts to hunt for her once they lose the tracking signal on the ship you destroyed. They will send more than three scouts next time."

"Agreed." I would trust my mate's safety to Prillon warriors who had been named outcast over an endless stream of mindless Hive slaves. There was no question.

Nial nodded to Warden Egara. "Send us to the Colony."

We stepped onto the transport platform and I looked at the darkly beautiful woman who had helped us save our mate, concerned that we left her behind unprotected. "Be careful once we are gone. The Hive might track our mate to you."

"I'm not afraid of those bastards." She looked fierce, filled with a rage I'd not seen in her before. I studied her with new eyes as she entered our destination in the control panel in front of her.

"You are brave and honorable. You would make an excellent bride." I knew several warriors who would be pleased with her darkly exotic hair and warm eyes.

"I already tried that. I'll pass." Her sad smile was the last thing I saw before the transport energy came for us.

CHAPTER NINE

Jessica

I was having the most amazing dream. Warm and comfortable, my bed was a mix of soft and firm. I rubbed my face against my pillow and the scent that rose, a dark, woodsy smell, made me smile. A hand stroked over my bare belly in slow and easy circles. It felt so good that I felt like I was melting and a contented sigh whispered past my lips.

"I will not begin her examination until she awakens."

I stiffened. I knew that voice. Nial's. But a stranger answered.

"I understand, prince, but a delay is dangerous. The others can scent her."

"She smells like Ander and me. Our seed is upon her."

"Regardless, it is not enough. She smells like an unmated female, and she does not wear a collar."

The conversation was alarming, but I didn't want to awaken. I didn't want to open my eyes or climb from my contented spot. And I did not want to deal with an examination or challenges. I did not want to wake up and face a room full of males trying to *sniff* me. Who cared what I smelled like? As far as I knew, I smelled like green tea shampoo and lavender-scented antiperspirant, as per the usual.

The strange voice continued, "On the Colony, an unmated female is unheard of and the warriors are demanding a chance to challenge for her."

"She is ours." Nial's voice boomed and startled me. My eyes flew open and I wasn't in a bed at all, but in his lap. I was staring at his massive chest, a gray shirt stretched taut over broad muscles. How I thought this pillow was soft was definitely part of a dream, for Nial—I knew it was Nial's lap without looking up at his face for I would recognize his scent anywhere—was all hard male. Everywhere, including the cock that nudged my hip.

"She is awake. As soon as she is examined and cleared for the claiming ceremony, we will remove her from the Colony. I assure you, doctor, we will not linger. She is hunted by the Hive."

Ander. I knew his voice now as readily as Nial's. He was loud and brash and direct, and very, very good with his tongue. I wondered if he did everything with the same intensity he used when he went down on me.

Nial's hand stilled on my belly. My bare belly. I glanced down and realized I was wrapped in another blanket, this one a dark red, not the bride processing center's dull gray. His hand had slipped between the folds to touch me directly. Warden Egara was nowhere to be seen, but a man wearing a gray uniform stood nearby, staring at me as if I were an alien. I did not recognize the room we were in. Blinking, I looked around Ander's large form, similarly clad in dark gray, and realized we weren't in the processing center at all.

"Where are we?" I asked. My voice was scratchy and I cleared my throat.

Nial gave me a gentle squeeze. "We are on the Colony, fourteen lightyears from Earth."

"The Colony?" I asked.

"It's a planet, near Earth. Coalition forces send all the

contaminated and non-functional warriors here to live out the remainder of their lives."

"What do you mean, contaminated?"

His body had tensed beneath me when he used that word, and I knew it pained him for some reason. I trusted my instincts, and they were screaming at me that his answer was important.

"The warriors who have been contaminated. Like me."

Confused, I stared at him. "You seem fine to me. Do you have a disease or something? What were you contaminated with? Radiation?"

"Hive technology." He lifted his hand and pointed to the left side of his face, the silver of his eye. "I have more, covering my back and leg."

Ander tensed as Nial spoke, watching me intently, as if my reaction mattered a great deal. I glanced to him for a brief moment. I hadn't seen Ander like this before without his face buried in my pussy. That was the only other time I'd seen him so serious, so intent. For a woman, that kind of focus, *there*, was a good thing. My pussy clenched at the thought of his skills.

I noticed the scar on the right side of *his* face. It was thick, running from the top of his forehead, down the outside of his eye socket, and farther down his cheek to his neck. I traced the path with my gaze, imagining a blade of some kind slicing through his flesh and decided I would have to kiss the entire length later, trace the scar with my tongue.

Nial's voice drew my attention from Ander and I turned to face him as he explained. "The Hive is our enemy, as it is Earth's. If a warrior, from any planet, is captured, they are *modified* into a Hive fighter. I was partially modified before being rescued. Nonetheless, to the Prillon Prime, my father, I am enough Hive to be contaminated."

His fingers squeezed my flesh, then relaxed.

"I am considered ruined on my world, an outcast, not worthy of a bride." He looked away from me, staring past me, and I frowned at his shame as he continued, "This is the reason my father refused your transport, Jessica. I carry Hive technology that can never be removed."

"So?" I lifted my hand to his cheek, to touch the silvery hued skin with my fingers. The softness of the oddly colored flesh was a shock, as was its warmth. But it was part of him, simple as that. "What does that have to do with anything?"

His stillness was unnatural and his gaze returned to my face. Beside us, the stranger I did not know had stopped moving as well, as if I'd shocked them all into silence. Confused, I turned to Ander and found his gaze smoldering, raw lust burning through his eyes to devour me. I shivered, unable to stop the flood of heat that made my core ache with emptiness as I met his gaze. I vividly remembered that same look as he'd sucked on my clit and made me scream. I shook my head, trying to clear the mixture of need and confusion I was feeling.

"You're all crazy. I don't think I want to go to Prillon, not if this is how you treat your vets." I thought of all my friends in the service who'd lost limbs, been burned by explosives, shot, hurt. They were good men and women, soldiers who had served with honor and deserved to be treated with care and respect when they returned home. I couldn't imagine sending a wounded veteran to what amounted to a prison colony, an outcast denied a mate and a family simply because a wound had altered their appearance. "What is wrong with you people? You should be ashamed if that's the way you treat your vets."

"What is a vet?" The strange man asked the question and I tore my gaze from Ander's to answer him.

"Who are you?" I wanted to know, since I was sitting half naked in the same room with him, and he seemed to think he had a right to be here.

"I am Doctor Halsen."

I inspected him then, noticed the same golden coloring and sharp angles of his face as Nial and Ander. His eyes were the color of bourbon on ice and his uniform was a strange green armor that looked more like forest camouflage than medical scrubs. He was also huge, close to seven feet tall. But whatever. As Dorothy would say, I wasn't in Kansas anymore.

"Vets is short for veterans. Soldiers who served and were then discharged."

He shook his head, confusion evident on his face. I sighed. I'd try again, in alien speak.

"Warriors who fought on the front lines. Some of them are wounded and sent home with honor. We call them veterans, and I'm one of them." I tugged on the blanket covering me as the doctor looked at me with confusion in his eyes.

"How is this possible? Females do not fight in war," he replied.

"Where I'm from, women fight. They work. They serve in the military and law enforcement. They don't sit on the sidelines and wait for a man to save them." I stared him down, pissed off by the way they treated their soldiers in general, and their misogynistic attitude in particular. All the macho testosterone in the room was making me see red. None of these aliens had earned my loyalty or my trust... well, none but Nial when he'd saved me from that Hive scout. Okay, perhaps Ander, too, when he got rid of the same scout.

The doctor took a step closer and I leaned back into Nial's arms, exceedingly aware of the fact that I was naked beneath the blanket.

"Fascinating. And you, *you* fought in a battle?" the doctor asked, but it was Ander who stepped forward, eager to hear my answer.

I nodded once. "Yes. Many times."

Nial's arms tightened around me, but I ignored him as I held the doctor's gaze, his disbelief evident in his raised brows and thin lips, even before he spoke. "I don't believe you."

I shoved at Nial and slid from his lap. If this alien jerk

really was a doctor, nothing I was about to show him should shock.

I stood proudly, the red blanket around my shoulders like a royal robe. I reached up and pulled my long hair forward over my shoulder so it wouldn't get in the way of what I was about to do. "I didn't get these scars baking cookies."

Without breaking eye contact, I dropped the blanket to the floor at my feet and spun around so he would see the ugly, ragged edged shrapnel scars that ran from my shoulder to my waist, across my buttock and onto my thigh. Ander stepped closer, his shoulders tense, but Nial held up his hand to prevent Ander's interference. Nial's gaze locked with mine as I glared at him with open defiance, daring him to stop me taking the pompous doctor down a notch.

I knew Nial could see the front of me, my breasts and pussy, but I didn't care. I should have questioned why I transported and arrived naked while Ander and Nial were clothed in identical shirts and pants. I'd ask later, but for now, I had something to prove.

Exposing my body was not to tease and lure the doctor. I heard him move and I spoke to the man without breaking eye contact with Nial. "Do not touch me."

Silence, then his voice, which held a previously absent note of awe and respect. "And so, it is true. You were wounded and sent home? You are one of the outcasts? The ones you call vet?"

I was going to strangle him. I spun around and lifted the blanket to cover myself. "Our vets are *not* outcasts. They are cared for and treated with respect. They resume their lives. We try to fully integrate them back into society. Many of them have families to go home to." At his confused look, I changed to alien speak again. "Mates and children waiting for their return."

"Your outcasts are allowed to claim mates?" Ander crouched beside me, staring up into my face with awe on his features. I leaned forward and placed my hand atop his scar on his cheek, traced the line with my fingertips as I'd imagined doing, letting him know his scar didn't make him less attractive to me.

"Some resent all soldiers, but mostly those people are angry about the wars on Earth, not at the soldier who fought. Most of our people treat all soldiers with great respect." I smiled as he shivered beneath my gentle exploration, and I recognized my actions as what they were, a claiming of my own. "Whether they were wounded or not."

The silence of the men around me was stifling and I pulled my hand back and cleared my throat. I looked around the oddly shaped room. It was circular, with dark glass of some sort from waist to ceiling. The floor was solid gray and smooth, like marble. I saw no door or exterior views. We could have been on a spaceship or hundreds of feet below ground. I had no way of knowing. "So, why are we here? Why did you bring me to this horrible place?"

The room wasn't horrible, but from what they said of the Colony, it wasn't Disneyland. I could only imagine what it was like outside the room's door.

"Do not worry, mate. We will only remain here long enough to ensure you are well," Ander promised. He rose to stand next to me, but he was so tall and bent at the waist so he could meet my eyes. "A ship is waiting to transport us to the battleship *Deston*. But before we leave you must be examined by the doctor to ensure you are well enough for the claiming ceremony."

I took stock of my body. The buckshot wounds no longer hurt. In fact, I felt as if it had never happened. I had no other complaints, although I did feel a little tender between my thighs. I flushed, thinking about how Ander's fingers had filled me. Fucked me. Brought me to orgasm again and again. No, that wasn't all. He'd also put his mouth on my pussy and licked my clit, sucked on it, flicked it, even nibbled on it until I came. The last memory I would have of Earth was being draped across Nial's lap in the processing center with both of my mates' mouths on me, making me come.

Oh, God, Earth. I was no longer on Earth. The thought was quick and fleeting because Ander stood over me and Nial moved to press his heat to my back. I was surrounded and I could no longer see the other man in the room. I didn't miss him. He had irritated me with his attitude, his questions about my abilities solely because I was a woman.

"I am well. I do not need to be checked by a doctor."

"You do," Ander countered. He straightened and moved to a table several steps behind Nial where I had not noticed it before. Ander placed his hands upon the hard surface. The doctor, still present, began to retrieve strange objects from shelves that lined one wall. As I looked around for the first time, I realized we were in an exam room and they had every intention of looking me over. All three of them.

This wasn't a *take a look at the scars on my back* kind of thing. This was a doctor's exam.

From the way Ander was staring at me, he wasn't going to change his mind. I tilted my chin to look up at Nial instead, hoping he'd see reason. "I'm fine. Really."

His lifted his hands to cup my face, tilting my head up to face him. "You were shot, Jessica, and healed by a decades-old ReGen wand. We should have waited to begin the bonding process, but we could not anticipate how strong your reaction would be. We gave you no chance to recover from our seed and transported you across the galaxy. We do not know if you were harmed in transport. I do not trust the ReGen wand that was used to mend your flesh or any internal damage that isn't visible. Also, we need to know the extent of your other injuries."

"What other injuries? I'm fine." I narrowed my eyes. What the hell was he talking about? I didn't have any other injuries.

"You carry many scars, my warrior bride. I do not know if you were completely healed from your war wounds. We need to know if you can safely carry a child. If we can fuck you the way we would like. You have accepted the seed placed upon you. The bonding has begun, but your reaction was very…" his eyes darkened with a look of desire I already recognized in my mate, "…extreme."

"Is that bad?" I asked, confused. They didn't like a woman who was passionate?

"We knew your body's response would be unique, but the sensations you experienced when we rubbed our essence into your skin will pale in comparison to the intensity of you will experience once we place our seed deep inside your body."

God, I'd have a freaking heart attack if it got much more intense. The thought made my breasts grow heavy and knew my mates would find a wet welcome between my legs.

Ander breathed deeply and nearly growled from across the room. He could smell how wet I was, damn it. How could they do that? I clenched my legs together, but it was futile, I knew.

"Sometimes we will take you more than once."

I shook my head, trying to make sense of everything that had happened to me in the last few hours. I remembered Nial holding me, touching me. I remember the shock of seeing Ander's mouth on my pussy, the heat of their seed as they'd taken their cocks in their own hands and drenched me with their primitive claim.

After that… things got fuzzy. I tried to remember which one of them had grabbed my thigh, which had sucked my nipples, whose hand had been in my hair and whose fingers in my core… but it all blurred into one thing… pleasure so intense I couldn't breathe. I'd been lost, drowning in it, drowning in these men. My men, if I believed their claims. My mates. I looked up to find Nial watching me closely.

"You still feel our connection, mate. Do not attempt to deny your desire. You screamed in my arms, your hoarse cries of pleasure still ring in my ears. And while it pleases me to know you are so… overcome by our connection, your reaction was not expected of a Prillon bride."

I flushed hotly. I could feel the heat of my blush coloring my face and neck. I didn't need to be reminded that I'd loved what they'd done to me. I'd loved every kiss, every caress. But to be told that my reaction was not normal confirmed what I already suspected. I was not princess material. If I couldn't handle the intensity of their alien seed on my skin, they should look elsewhere for a bride. I'd lost control and... I must have lost consciousness for I remembered nothing else. And they hadn't even fucked me!

They'd given me orgasm after orgasm and it had been so intense, I lost myself completely. I had forgotten where I was, and hadn't cared. I'd been out of control, and that was dangerous. I would have let them do anything to me.

Anything. I probably would have even begged them for more.

"That doesn't mean I should be looked at. It just means you're good," I ground out the last, admitting the way he and Ander affected me. If I were going to be looked at, it should be by a shrink. No woman should feel so strongly attached to two men she'd barely met. No woman should have allowed them to do what they'd done to me. No, not allowed. Begged for more.

"We have not fucked you yet," Ander said, as if I needed reminding. "But we will. Soon."

I glanced at the doctor and gave Ander a warning look, but he did not seem embarrassed as I was.

"I'm fine."

"If you are so... overcome by just my fingers and mouth, by our seed splattered across your belly and breasts, then it is possible we could harm you when you take our cocks."

"Ander," I ground out, really wishing he'd shut up about now.

"He speaks the truth," Nial added. "It is our job to protect you, not harm you. We must make sure you are healthy enough to claim properly."

He stood, taking me in his arms, and lifted me upon the exam table.

"What do you mean, properly?"

What could there be, other than fucking? Which, if I were being completely honest with myself, I wasn't totally opposed to the idea of riding Nial's huge cock, or taking both of them in my mouth in turns, tasting their seed as an orgasm roared through my body.

"This is the second time I've been examined." The table was similar to the one in the processing center where the warden had removed the pieces of metal from my back and thigh and used that amazing healing wand. "If there was something wrong with me, Warden Egara would have found it."

"Not true," Ander said. "We gave you our seed, we gave you our pleasure after."

His big hands opened the blanket to expose my body to the doctor. But with my anger gone, I found weathering his inspection unbearable. I did not want the doctor to look at me, let alone touch me.

"Ander!" I scrabbled to grab the blanket, but he took hold of my wrists and moved to stand at the top of the table, pulling me into a reclined position, my wrists snugly held within one of his large palms. With my arms over my head as they were, my back arched and my breasts thrust upwards.

Looking up, I narrowed my eyes at the brute.

"Let me go!"

Slowly, he shook his head. "You will be seen to. It is our job to ensure your safety and well-being."

Nial stood at my side and tilted his head. "We are going to fuck you, Jessica. Often and thoroughly. The doctor is going to ensure you can handle your mates' demands."

Ander sniffed the air. "Can you smell her?"

Nial flicked his gaze to Ander. "Yes. Interesting."

I squirmed against Ander's hold, but I knew it was futile. I did it anyway. The doctor, damn him, remained quiet at the foot of the table. Clearly he was waiting for permission to begin.

"What the hell is interesting?" I asked.

Nial arched a brow at my angry tone. *He* wasn't the one being pinned down naked in front of a total stranger. "What is interesting, mate, is that you are aroused by this."

"I am not!" I retorted, but my nipples pebbled into hard peaks. I clenched my thighs together tightly in defiance. Perhaps if I closed them, my mates wouldn't be able to smell just what Ander's firm hold was doing to my body. The logic behind it was completely ridiculous and it baffled me. Somehow, deep down I knew that if these mates were going to claim me, I needed to know they were stronger than I. I'd spent my life protecting other people and had yet to meet a man who made me feel like he could truly do a better job protecting me than I could myself.

Ander could hold me down, keep me held exactly where he wanted me with just one firm grip. This domination made part of me angry, made me want to fight, to challenge his hold. The other part of me, however, the part I'd kept buried deep in my soul, the screaming girl who wanted to feel like the world was a safe place again? She was waking up now, hoping to be set free. The more I fought her, the wilder she became inside me until my need for Ander's dominant touch created a civil war between my heart and mind. I bucked on the table and my heart pounded so loudly I was sure the hammering could be heard in the next room.

I needed to know that no matter what I did, Ander would be there, strong enough to control me, to control the world about me.

Nial placed a thick black strap over my squirming hips and cinched it to the table so I could no longer lift them. When I kicked out, he lifted both of my legs into stirrups the doctor had raised from beneath the table. No doubt he'd kept them hidden, for if I'd seen them earlier, I would have bolted for the door. They, of course, were similar to those at my gynecologist's office and Nial strapped my ankles to the thick metal. When he was done, he looked at Ander.

"Do you require straps for her arms?"

Ander chuckled and leaned down to breathe his answer into my ear. "No. I *enjoy* holding her down."

Oh, God. That made me really hot.

Nial grinned and used a strange crank of some kind to adjust the stirrups, spreading my legs wide, my bare pussy on display, the edge of my ass practically hanging off the table. Instead of the doctor, Nial stepped between my legs and slid one long finger into my pussy as I panted.

"She is so wet, Ander. We could take her now, spread her wet juices on our cocks, and take her hard and fast."

Ander's hands tensed on my wrists, but he did not hurt me. I wanted to squirm, but even that small act of defiance was denied me by the heavy strap over my hips. I was so angry I wanted to spit at Nial and scratch out his eyes, and so turned on I hoped he would drop his pants and fuck me while Ander held me down and watched.

What the hell was wrong with me?

Nial turned to the doctor and nodded before stepping away, giving the doctor room to do whatever he was going to do to me. I had no hope of escaping whatever they had planned.

I watched as Nial licked my pussy juice from his finger, rolling his tongue around the tip as if I tasted like the sweetest honey.

Determined not to surrender, I turned back to watch the doctor's approach. He looked resigned, completely clinical. I saw no arousal, not eagerness in his gaze, which helped. Yet when he held up the two dildos in his hands, I arched my back and doubled my efforts to break Ander's iron hold.

CHAPTER TEN

Nial

I watched as the doctor approached my mate. Her defiance was beautiful to behold. I'd always imagined myself with a docile, submissive queen, but now thanked the gods and the matching process protocols for giving me such a hellion, a warrior who wasn't afraid to fight, and wasn't intimidated by her mates' scars.

"No way. What the hell do you think you're doing?" she shouted at the doctor, but he ignored her protests and settled his supplies on the small partition he pulled out from the side of the table. "What kind of exam involves... those things?"

He lifted a hand to her thigh, but she bucked and fought Ander so fiercely I feared she would burst a blood vessel in her heart if we did not calm her down. The medical equipment was necessary to her survival on Prillon. Not only did I need to be sure she wasn't injured by our need to fully claim her, but because I had taken her from Earth without proper processing, she lacked the fundamental biological implants she would need to live a happy and healthy life on Prillon.

I held up my hand and the doctor backed away. Jessica was gasping for air as I approached her side. "Jessica, please. We are not going to hurt you. The doctor is following standard protocol. All brides go through the same testing process. I promise you this. Trust me. I would not allow him to harm you in any way."

"Bullshit. This is bullshit. No medical exam requires dildos, you perverted assholes. Let me go!" She fought hard and the system monitoring her blood pressure and heart rate started to peal with alarm bells.

"She needs to calm down. She could have a stroke." The doctor's words caused me grave concern and I knew it was time to show my new mate the true meaning of Prillon discipline.

I walked to her and placed my hand on her chest. "Calm down, Jessica. The exam is necessary. Stop fighting us or I'm going to spank your bottom until it's burning red."

She glared at me, her back arching up off the table as she tried to twist free of Ander's hold. "What? Like I'm a three-year-old? No. Let me go."

"Trust us, mate. The doctor will not hurt you." Ander tried to help our cause. "I promise you, if he hurts you, he dies."

"No." She fought, turning her head and craning her neck trying to bite my arm so I would release her.

"I warned you, Jessica. Now you will be taught what it means to defy your mate." I lifted my arm and walked to the bottom of the table where her perfectly round bottom was on display, her legs spread wide and secured by the straps. I ran my palm over her smooth, round flesh in a soft caress to be sure she knew where I was, and where I planned to strike her. "I'm going to spank you now because you refused to listen. When it comes to your health or your safety, Jessica, I will not be denied."

I met and held her gaze and she calmed her breathing enough to speak to me. "Don't you dare."

I struck hard and fast; her scream one of anger, not pain.

"That's one."

"Asshole."

"That will cost you another strike of my hand, Jessica. You'd best learn to watch your mouth." I struck her in earnest then, turning her ass a fiery shade of red, deeply satisfied as her verbal barrage faded to silent rage, her pink pussy glistening with wet welcome as I inspected her folds, giving her time to adjust to her new position and accept me as her master, her true mate.

As expected, the pause in my lessons brought her fire back to the surface. "Is that it? Because if it is, you can fuck off now and let me up. I'm still not letting that doctor fuck me with his sex toys like a pervert."

I met Ander's gaze and nodded to be sure he knew to tighten his grip. Sliding two fingers into her wet pussy, I used the other to stroke her clit as I fucked her with them, bringing her to the edge, the peak of a release, before withdrawing. "This is just the beginning of your lesson, since you still speak to your mate with such disrespect."

Her moan of anguished pleasure pleased me as I watched her pussy clench around open air, desperate for what I denied her. "You will count this time, Jessica. Count to twenty as I punish you for defying me. When we are done, I will invite the doctor over to continue his exam."

"I don't want the exam." Her chest was heaving, her beautiful body on display for us. It was all I could do not to drop my pants and fuck her right there, on the edge of the table. But that was not why we were here. She needed the biological implants the doctor would provide, and she needed to be cleared as healthy before Ander and I could fully take her. I did not want to wait because she was too stubborn to allow the standard medical examination.

"I know. But it's necessary. You will allow him to care for you, or I will spank you until you see reason. Do you understand?"

"Go to hell."

I pushed three fingers into her pussy, hard and deep,

tickling the tip of her womb as she arched her back with a soft cry and the walls of her pussy clamped down on my fingers in welcome. I rubbed her clit until she whimpered, but did not let her come. She would surrender to me in all ways, or she would not leave this table.

"Don't forget to count, Jessica." I slid my fingers free and resumed spanking her naked bottom. I was to three before she began to count.

"Three."

"Start at one, mate. We will begin at one."

She shuddered as I struck her again, but her voice whispered the word I wanted to hear.

"One."

Smack.

"Two."

Smack.

I continued to twenty, her ass a beautiful shade of red and her pulse racing. She quivered, her back arching as tears streamed from the corners of her eyes. Her voice had changed to shuddering sobs as I finished, but she was calm and submissive in Ander's hold.

I resumed my place beside her, my large palm spread over her chest as she stared off to the side, not meeting my gaze. "Are you ready to allow the doctor to examine you now, mate?"

"I don't understand why I have to do this."

She wasn't happy, but she was listening. "The doctor must test your nervous system to make sure it is functioning properly. There are some implants you need to live on our world. He will also test your fertility and make sure you do not carry any diseases."

"What is that? What implants?" She shuddered as she waited for my answer. The truth was, I wasn't sure exactly how it all worked, so I turned to the doctor.

"Doctor? Please answer my mate's question."

The doctor took one step forward, but Jessica jerked in Ander's hold so he stopped where he was to speak. "You have not been implanted with full Prillon bioprocessing units. That must also be done."

"What does that mean?"

The doctor nodded his head. "Our technology recycles all matter into its base form. The clothing we wear, the food we eat, and the waste produced by our bodies is all reclaimed and used by our systems. Prillon children are given the proper implants at birth. However, since you are from Earth and did not complete the full processing before your... aborted transport, you do not have the necessary implants required for life on our battleships." He spread his hands wide and took a hesitant step forward. "On my honor as a Prillon warrior and doctor, I mean you no harm."

"Fine. Do what you have to do." She closed her eyes and turned her head away, her jaw tense but her arms relaxed beneath Ander's hold. He leaned over our bride and kissed her softly, his lips stealing her tears from her cheek.

"Good girl, Jessica. Don't worry, mate. I will keep you safe. You have my word."

I took my place at Jessica's side, keeping the doctor within reach and Jessica's soft, pink pussy within view. I trusted the good doctor, but only so far. We were on the Colony, and I wasn't completely sure of his loyalty. One wrong move, one flicker of desire in his eyes, and I'd rip his head from his shoulders. He looked at me with the first instrument held aloft. I placed my hand on Jessica's thigh so she would know I stood watch over her.

"Begin, doctor."

The doctor pulled the swollen lips of Jessica's pussy wide, baring her center to me and I could not tear my gaze from the sight as he prepared to insert a long, thick scanner into her body that would test her fertility and scan for disease. An adjustable secondary attachment was meant to test my mate's nervous system and reaction to sexual stimuli, but that was not yet connected to Jessica's sensitive clit. I knew she functioned perfectly, her response to Ander's mouth on her there all the proof I required.

However, the protocols must be met else she would not be accepted as a Prillon bride. She wouldn't be any Prillon bride; she'd be a Prillon princess.

The doctor pressed forward, the thick device just entering my mate's wet pussy, stretching her open to accept the sizable probe. Jessica's soft moan made me go rock hard as the long device, nearly the size of my own cock, slowly disappeared between her greedy pink folds. A data recording station on the wall began to display numbers and other information I didn't understand, but the doctor scanned the data and nodded with approval before reaching for the second device, which I knew was meant for Jessica's ass. This one was much smaller than Ander's cock, and would be used to gauge her readiness to be fucked by both of her mates at once, which was the only way to be truly bonded.

I ran my hand along Jessica's soft thigh because she needed to know I was with her, and because I needed to touch her, remind myself she was real and she was mine. I needed this exam to be over with as quickly as possible.

We needed the doctor to issue our mating collars, and he wouldn't do so until Jessica was cleared by her medical exam. Without my collar around her neck, all unmated males on the Colony would believe they had the right to challenge me for her.

And challenge me they would. Already I could hear the warriors gathering, milling around on the other side of the glass watching as my beautiful mate was examined. It was their right to bear witness, and I had no doubt at least one would issue a challenge. The only question on my mind was how many of them Ander and I would have to kill before we got our mate off this planet.

• • • • • • •

Jessica

I was strapped to the exam table, held open and exposed as the doctor inserted a giant dildo into my soaking wet pussy. I didn't know what else to expect, but Ander's hold on my wrists had not lessened, and now Nial's rough hand stroked my inner thigh, up and down, as if he were petting a kitten.

I didn't understand what had just happened to me, but my bottom was sore, I was utterly humiliated and so desperate for Nial's touch, for his calm control, that I longed to crawl off the exam table and into his arms. For the first time in days, perhaps weeks, my mind was calm and clear, my fear gone. I felt at peace.

Years of conditioning made me think I should be angry at his treatment of me, of his punishment and demand for obedience. Instead, his touch simply made me hungry for more, made me wish the doctor would leave us alone so I could have Nial's thick cock in my body instead of the hard probe. I had experienced the bliss of their bonding seed once, and already I craved it with a desperate need that would have embarrassed me were I not dealing with much more humiliating things at the moment. Like the doctor's finger exploring the tight virgin opening of my ass, and pushing inside with something warm and viscous coating his finger.

I gasped.

I knew what lube felt like, but instead of the cold jelly I was used to at my doctor's office, this liquid felt like warm oil that flowed into my ass, coating my insides with a substance that made me feel even more sensitive.

As the round head of a second device began to breach my body I realized that holding my eyes closed was poor strategy. Indeed, all it did was make me focus on every single detail, the smallest sensation of the moment could not escape my notice. I could count the speed of Ander's breath and hear the racing of his heart. Nial's stance beside me felt cautious and alert, and oddly proud, as if he were showing off my pussy to the masses like a trophy.

The doctor, however clinical, was doing things to me I'd never experienced before. As the strange device slid into my bottom, I clenched my ass, trying to prevent its entry. Fighting it.

Nial slapped my inner thigh with one swift, sharp strike and I gasped with shock as fire raced through my bloodstream. "Stop fighting him, Jessica. Let him do what needs to be done so we can go."

I opened my eyes to find Ander staring down at me with such raw need in his eyes that I froze, unable to deny him.

"You have a virgin ass, don't you?" His question was dark and deep.

I blushed and nodded.

He growled deep in his chest in reply.

I licked my lips. "Ander. Distract me."

He smiled. God, he was so handsome. His strong jaw, penetrating eyes, feral gaze. I could get lost just looking at him, but that wasn't enough.

"With pleasure." Rising, he adjusted his hold on my arms so he could walk to the side of the table opposite Nial and lean over me. Even before he'd settled into his new position, he lowered his head and kissed me like a man possessed. His kiss set me on fire and I relaxed as the doctor stretched me open, sliding the second object into my body in slow, measured thrusts until I was stuffed so full I felt like I was going to explode if they didn't either make me come or let me go.

As Ander kissed me, Nial used his free hand to cup one of my breasts, tug on the nipple and squeeze just hard enough to make me arch up into his commanding hold. His second hand drifted down from my thigh to my clit, exploring the edges, teasing me until I began to fight Ander's hold once more, not because I wanted up off the table, but because I needed more than they were allowing me to have.

Nial's thick fingers spread my pussy lips wide around the dildo and Ander's tongue plunged deep just as I felt a strange extraction device settle over my clit. It wasn't Nial's lips or mouth, for I knew what a warrior's mouth felt like sucking on me until I screamed. This felt odd, like a suction cup made of soft rubber. I tried to tear my mouth from Ander's to ask, but he denied me that freedom, leaning more fully onto my upper body until I felt trapped beneath his giant frame. Pinned, not just by the straps or his hands, but by the sheer brute size and strength of him.

For some reason I didn't care to examine, the sensation made me go wild. I forgot about the doctor and his stupid exam. All I cared about was my two big warriors, their hands and mouths, and the hard, thick invasion of my pussy. And ass. I couldn't deny that while uncomfortable, it only heightened the feelings that were coursing through me.

Nial replaced his hand on my nipple with his mouth and the doctor must have switched something on, because the sucking sensation on my clit increased in speed. Suck. Release. Harder. Release.

It began to vibrate as well and Nial reached between my legs, pulling the big, long dildo from my pussy, plunging it back in.

He increased his pace, fucking me with the thing as the secondary machine worked my clit with a programmed mastery that left me on the precipice. It was as if the machine knew when I was going to have an orgasm, and shut down at the last possible moment to prevent my release.

It went on and on. When the doctor began fucking me with the dildo in my ass I whimpered beneath Ander's mouth, unable to do anything but surrender to the moment and the desperation that spiraled out of control in my body.

I was no longer myself. I was nothing but a body, a bundle of nerves and lust without name or memory. I was my mates' to do with as they wished. It was a scary concept, but their sole intent was to give me pleasure.

Ander released me from his kiss and I turned my head to the side, trying to catch my breath as both objects plunged in and out of my body, the vibrating clit suction increasing in strength and speed.

I opened my eyes to find myself inches from Nial's intense gaze as he loomed over me. "Do you wish to come, mate?" He pulled the dildo almost completely from my body, holding it at my entrance in a deliberate tease.

I practically sobbed. So empty. I was so very empty. "Yes."

"Ask nicely, Jessica." He plucked my nipple, hard enough to hurt and my pussy clamped down on nothing in a spasm that was actually painful.

"Please." I stared into his gold and silver eyes, and I gave him what he wanted, that one word a chant that consumed me. "Please. Please. Please."

One of Ander's hands slid from my wrist down the long line of my arm to my shoulder to settle like a warm blanket over my throat, not squeezing, nothing more than reminding me that I was his, under his complete control, and there was nothing I could do but submit.

"Come for us. Come now." Nial's voice had gone deeper than I'd ever heard it, his words an undeniable command.

My body responded instantly, the explosion racing over me as I screamed my release. Once I started, I couldn't seem to stop, for the moment I thought to come down, Ander would force my mouth open to taste and explore, Nial and the doctor would fuck me with their devices, and the suction on my clit would increase, tugging on my body, vibrating with enough power to make my back arch up off the table as I came apart again and again.

I had no idea how long it lasted, but I was dripping with sweat and worn out when it was over. Ander stroked my hair back from my face and Nial stood like a guard over my body, his hand never leaving me, constantly touching my abdomen, my thigh, so I would know he was near.

"Well, doctor?" Nial's clipped question forced me from my daze. I wanted to know what the doctor had to say about all of *that*.

"She did very well, my prince." He slipped the dildo in my pussy from me, the odd piece over my clit going away with it. "Her body's response levels are actually quite a bit better than most Prillon brides."

I wanted to roll my eyes, but settled for closing them as Nial removed my legs from the stirrups and unstrapped my hips.

"And were the implants successful? Is she ready to transport to the battleship?" Ander's touch turned extremely gentle as he massaged both of my temples where the neurostims were placed. He buried his hands in my hair and gently kneaded my scalp.

"Yes. The implants are fully operational."

I forgot all about that part of the exam. While I'd been pleasured, he'd put the Prillon implants in me. Somewhere. God, an orgasm was much better than anesthetic.

"She is ready."

I opened my eyes and frowned. "Um, I think you forgot something," I told him, then embarrassingly pointed down between my legs where the hard object was still in my bottom.

Nial, with the slightest of touches, slid a finger down my slit to bump the object. "No. This plug will remain in your ass."

I came up onto my elbows. "What? Why?"

"Because you must be stretched there for our cocks. We will take you... together, Jessica."

"You have yet to see my cock," Ander said and I turned to look at him. "I assure you it is much larger than that plug. Nial will take your pussy, as is his sole right as your primary mate. I will not fuck you there until you carry his child. But I *will* take your ass, as is my right and privilege as your second."

I thought of Ander's cock and had to assume it was as big as the rest of him. I clenched down on the foreign object that filled me deep and opened me up. I couldn't close up and I felt... full. What would Ander's cock be like instead?

"I don't want this thing inside me. It's uncomfortable," I commented.

"Is it hurting you?" Ander asked, worry changing his demeanor. "Doctor," he growled.

I had no doubt Ander would break the man's neck if the plug he'd inserted was harming me.

I held up my hand. "No, do not harm him. It doesn't hurt. It's just… odd. I've never had anything—" I cleared my throat, "—there before."

Ander smiled then. "Knowing I will be the first pleases me, mate. The plug will remain in, and every time you feel the hard length stretching you open, imagine me fucking you there, imagine my cock filling you as Nial's takes your pussy."

His words filled me with a dangerous heat as I imagined riding Nial's hard cock, lifting my ass, baring myself so Ander could take me as well, so he could fill me to the breaking point, until I lost control.

I wasn't an innocent. I'd watched enough porn to know exactly what he was talking about, and the thought of being between two such powerful men made my body clench down on the plug. I bit my lip, looking away as my pussy grew wet once more. I wanted to please him, and didn't mind leaving the plug in my ass. I wanted them to fuck me, to share me and stuff me completely full of both their cocks. If walking around with this thing inside me for a while would get me what I wanted, I'd do so.

The oddity here was my desire to let them both take me. I was a modern, successful, liberated woman. I didn't bow down to men and I didn't take any bullshit from anyone, either. So why did the thought of being completely dominated by both of my mates at once make me so damn hot? The idea of surrendering total control to anyone was anathema. Submitting to a spanking, something that just a few days ago I would have battled with every last breath in my body.

Now that I had tasted the oblivion of giving them

control, I knew I would crave that kind of release again and again. Hell, maybe I'd always had. But until Nial and Ander, until now, there had never been a man I thought worthy, someone strong enough, someone stronger than I, to whom I would even consider surrender.

My thoughts surprised me, for I would have *never* submitted to a man in such a way before. I *wanted* to be free to let go. I wanted to know I could trust them to take care of me. And, even more shocking, I wanted to please them both. I wanted them insane with longing for me, for the pleasure they would take in my body. I wanted to be everything they needed. Everything.

The doctor held out three long black ribbons, which Nial took, making a fist around them. "Thank you."

The doctor actually looked nervous then and I thought I heard something, a thumping sound, like people fighting, on the other side of the walls as he spoke. "I'd hurry if I were you."

Nial turned to me and held out his hand to Ander, who took one of the strips and lifted it to his neck. Nial did the same, laying the third on the table next to me. I wondered why they were donning black chokers, but as I watched, they both turned a deep, dark red and seemed to melt into the men's skin so that they looked more like a tattoo than a collar.

Nial picked up the third as Ander helped me to sit, carefully with the thing in my bottom. "For you, mate."

I reached for the black strip in his hand with trembling fingers. "What is it?"

"Our bonding collar. This marks you as ours for the claiming period. No other warriors may approach you or try to steal you from us. The collars will link us as one, a family."

I looked at the seemingly innocent strip of black in my hand and realized exactly what I was holding. This was their version of a wedding ring. Permanent claim. A big fat mark on a woman's body that said *taken*.

And they hadn't even asked. Seriously? I wasn't one of those girls that expected a big production out of a wedding proposal, but it would have been nice to at least be asked. What happened to the whole, *I love you and want to be with you forever* speech? After what they'd just done to me—or rather, what they'd allowed the doctor to do to me—I wasn't in the mood to be forced or coerced into anything else. I had a plug in my ass because they wanted it there, and because I was honest enough about my own desires to know that I wanted to take them both, at least once. But this…?

I closed my fist around the collar and lowered it to my lap. "No."

He glowered as the doctor stepped back mumbling about challenges and killing. I could have tried harder to listen, but I was too busy staring down two big, bossy aliens.

"Put it on, now." Nial's lips thinned and his eyes narrowed as he tried to intimidate me into obeying him. "Jessica, by Prillon law I cannot force you to wear my collar. However, if you do not put it around your neck right now, you will be placing yourself at risk."

I glared right back. Seriously? He'd just let a doctor double penetrate me with a couple of dildos and a magical suction cup in sexual fantasy land, and he expected me to say yes to a proposal he'd never made? I looked around the room. Nope. No big hulking monsters waiting to strike me down for refusing his non-proposal. Just me, my mates, and the doctor, who'd already done just about everything he could do to me. I would not be bullied into obeying. Not for this.

"Where I'm from, when a man *asks* a woman, and let me repeat that one critically important word here, *asks* a woman to be his bride, he usually gets down on one knee and gives her a damn good reason to say yes."

Nial's brow went up, but that was it. "Put the collar on."
"No."
"Put the collar around your neck, right now."
"Ask nicely, Nial."

I threw his own words back in his face and crossed my arms beneath my naked breasts. I was over being embarrassed by my nudity and sat like a queen holding court. There was nothing on this body that all three men in this room hadn't seen aplenty and my pussy and ass still tingled and throbbed from the release. Surely the table was slick and wet beneath where I sat.

Ander rose from his place beside me and faced what appeared to be a doorway, ignoring me as Nial's silver eye turned jet black. I didn't care if he was angry. I was, too.

First I'd been denied transport by his stupid father, tracked by the Hive and nearly killed by my old mentor. Nial had saved my life, but he'd tricked me into being with both of them right after I'd been shot. Then they had taken me from my planet, tied me down, spanked me, and fucked me with strange medical equipment and forced me to lose control of myself in front of a total stranger. I rolled with the punches, adapting to the situation. I had gone along with everything they had wanted, despite my own better judgment. I was not going to agree to marry these two cavemen if they didn't even *ask* me!

I glared right back at him waiting for him to figure out what I wanted, what I needed from him. His shoulders dropped and his eye changed back to silver as he stared at me. "What do you want, Jessica?"

The defeat I saw in his eyes nearly made me relent, but damn it! I wanted a real proposal. After everything they'd put me through already, I at least deserved that. It wasn't like I was going to say no. I had no home and no life to go back to. If I went home—which was probably impossible anyway—I'd be dead in less than a week.

And I'd miss these two warriors as well, as much as it pained me to admit that, even to myself. I'd only known them a few hours, but already they felt like they were mine.

I was staring into Nial's confused eyes, trying to figure out how to tell him what I needed without sounding like an overly sentimental idiot, when the door burst off its frame and two huge warriors invaded the room.

The bigger one was covered in the same silvery skin my Nial had, but his silver covered his chest and neck, not his face. His eyes were a warm honey brown but he had an odd metallic attachment imbedded in his flesh just above his right eye, like a second eyebrow. He didn't even look in my direction, but directly at Nial.

"I challenge for the right to claim this Earth woman as my bride."

CHAPTER ELEVEN

Jessica

Nial seemed to grow several inches taller, his silver skin sparkling under the slight blue tinge of the exam room lighting. "Touch her and I will kill you."

Another man, one I realized now was the challenger's second, moved along the edge of the room, toward me… and Ander, who positioned himself in front of me. The one moving toward us looked completely normal, for an alien, until I looked into his eyes. They were both lined with silver rings, like a jeweler had wrapped matching wedding bands around his irises.

Contaminated. The word floated through my mind until I heard Nial's roar.

Turning quickly, I saw Nial lift the other warrior over his head like a weightlifting bar and hurl him sideways into a piece of black glass more than twenty feet across the room. The glass, or whatever it was, shattered and fell to the floor with a loud cracking and tinkling sound and I gasped as row upon row of warriors were revealed to me where they must have been standing the entire time.

Watching *everything*. Oh, my God, they'd seen me being

spread open and spanked and fucked and my orgasm and my pleasure and…

Ander waited for his attacker to charge as Nial's roar literally shook the remaining windows. Ander drew back and planted his fist squarely in the challenger's jaw, sending him sprawling, unconscious several feet back from where he'd started his attack. One punch and the man was down.

Nial and Ander looked at each other and positioned themselves around me. I looked up to see another pair of warriors nod to each other and enter the room through the broken doorway. They were huge, equal in size to my mates, but much more cautious than the first two had been.

I stared at the black strip of ribbon in my hand and gave in to the inevitable. I understood now the urgency, the doctor's warning. All of it. I knew I wanted my mates, I just wanted them to desire me with more than their bodies. I wanted their hearts. I wanted a true connection.

That kind of love took time. I knew that. In the meantime, I did not want my mates to have to fight the entire Colony to get me out of here. And I definitely did not want to take the chance that they might lose a challenge, or be seriously hurt, although that did not seem to be much of a problem.

With a sigh I looked at the giant lurking in the doorway. "Stop."

All four warriors froze, as did the doctor and the men still milling about on the other side of the wall.

I lifted the strange collar to my neck and let go, surprised when it locked itself in place around my neck.

Instantly, I was flooded with battle rage and a fierce need to protect what was mine. I realized the feelings were coming from both of my mates and I lifted my shaking hand to my neck with wonder. There would be no lying, no games. I would know what they felt when they were near.

As I lowered my hand, the large intruder bowed low and held up his hands to ward off Nial's strike. "My apologies, princess."

Perhaps Nial's fierce orders had not been because he lacked romance, but because he actually feared for my safety. They'd vowed to protect me with their lives, to knock out, hurt, or even kill any male that would get near me. The one person they couldn't protect me from was myself. They were willing to take on every male in the Colony if need be, but they couldn't force me to put the collar about my neck.

In a backwards sort of way, they had been showing me how much they cared.

I looked at Nial, and the others, noting their complete change in attitude since I'd placed the collar around my neck. Nial hadn't been exaggerating the danger to me, and I suddenly felt foolish for denying him and risking all of our lives. I spoke directly to Nial's challenger.

"No, I am the one who is sorry. My lack of understanding caused this mess, but I am not interested in any men but my mates."

Ander backed toward me, as did Nial, completely cutting off my view of the two men who had barged into the room. The doctor knelt on the floor next to the warrior Nial had thrown into the window and I sighed in relief when I saw the warrior's arm move. He wasn't dead. Good. That was a dose of guilt I did not need.

The challenger's second spoke for the first time. "Are there other women like you on Earth, princess? Women who might be willing to mate with a contaminated veteran, as you called us?"

I sighed. Single women looking for smoking hot, honorable warriors? "Absolutely. Thousands and thousands of them, but you are *not* contaminated."

The doctor coughed. "Gods, my prince, you had best get her out of here immediately. She's going to launch an invasion of Earth."

"What?" I wondered. "I'm not either. All I have to do is call—or whatever it is you do from space—Warden Egara. She'll help them find mates once I explain the situation to her. She takes her job very seriously. Trust me. She'll be happy to help."

How I knew this, I wasn't sure, but I was completely confident that I spoke the truth.

The warrior at the door tilted his head. "Lady Egara of the battleship *Wothar*? Catherine?"

I shoved at Ander's arm so he would move aside a couple of inches. I needed to see this man's face. "I don't know her first name and I know nothing of a battleship. I'm fairly positive she's never been to space, for I've been told that no woman ever returns to Earth once matched."

"She would be smaller than you, princess, with dark hair and gray eyes?"

"That sounds like her." I frowned at him. "How do you know her?"

"She was mate to my brother and his second. They were both killed six years ago in an ambush. We lost an entire battle group that day." He nodded at his second and pointed to his own silver skin. "The rest of us were recovered several hours later, but we didn't get to go home."

He meant that they had all been sent to the Colony instead because of their new *contamination*.

Nial stepped out of sight then reappeared with my dark red blanket, which he draped over me before lifting me into his arms. I realized I'd been naked as I had a conversation with two complete strangers. With a plug in my butt. *God.*

"I can walk, you know."

He shook his head. "Not today. Today you cause too much trouble even when your feet do not touch the ground."

I chuckled at that and he looked to Ander.

"Let's go, Ander. It is time."

Ander fell into step beside us and the others bowed as Nial carried me past them all out into a long corridor lined with doors. I wrapped my arms around his neck and leaned my head on his shoulder, allowing him to take me where he willed. "Where are we going now? Time for what?"

"Time to teach you exactly what it means to be a bride

of Prillon."

• • • • • • •

Nial

I carried my mate down the long, plain corridor and felt rage gather in my chest. I was supposed to live the rest of my life on the Colony. It was to be my new home. This place, these men, were supposed to be my future—if my father had his way. The men who we'd just fought, those who wanted Jessica for their own, were like me. Warriors who had fought for the coalition, protected billions of lives on hundreds of planets, but unlucky enough to be captured and tortured by the Hive, *contaminated* by their technology and banished forever.

Shame at my lack of understanding made me clench my jaw as I carried my mate. Jessica had pointed out the obvious, that there was nothing wrong with any of them. Their Hive biotech implants were like her scars: marks of honor, of service. Of respect. If anything, the implanted technology would make them all stronger, faster, and more lethal than ever before. And yet these men found themselves banished to the Colony, disrespected and forgotten. Denied a mate, denied a family. Stripped of their honor and their worth and used for nothing more than slave labor.

The disgraceful treatment of our warriors would be one of the first things I would change once I was Prime. I looked down at the golden shimmer of my mate's hair where she rested in my arms and knew, without doubt, my princess would be a fierce advocate for these warriors as well.

It had been a proud moment for me to see her confront the doctor, confront injustice, and make us all see things in a new light. Her words, her ideals, were meant to protect not just the two men who would claim her, but all the veterans of the Hive wars, all the wounded and scarred warriors on this world. I had no doubt she would fight my father's prejudiced system, without surcease. She was fierce and brave and passionate.

My perfect mate.

It was time now to claim her, to fuck her. We *should* be fleeing the Colony without pause, but I had to fuck her first. She had to understand the power of our mating bond and a good, hard fuck would do that in ways words could not. The collars, as well as a few intense orgasms, would ensure that she never doubted our bond again.

This wouldn't be the ceremonial bonding, our permanent claiming, but it would be a start. With the collars about our necks, with our seed having coated her skin, her emotions and needs were obvious now. I sensed her every feeling as she felt mine—and Ander's—in kind.

I felt the lingering arousal from her examination. She'd liked it. Loved it. Loved fighting against Ander's hold, knowing that there was nothing she could do but give in. Despite the unfamiliar situation, she'd chosen to trust Ander, to have faith that he would not allow anything harmful to happen to her while he'd gripped her wrists. She had taken comfort in our presence, trusted us and been able to submit to the examination. I had never seen anything more beautiful than her orgasms as Ander and I held her, watched over her.

She'd lost control, and that had just been to the medical probes. I longed to discover how loudly she might scream her release when it was Ander and I fucking her, stretching her, making her come.

One of the men led us down a hallway and pressed a button on a wall, three, no four doors down. He bowed once. "A privacy chamber."

I nodded to the man, who, only a few minutes ago, Ander had punched in the face. There was no animosity among us, for the authority and respect for mates of our warriors was strong, the collar around her neck a permanent sign of ownership. She owned us now. Both of us would die to protect our right to care for her, father her children, and bring her pleasure.

Ander thanked the man and closed the door behind us. I took in the room. A bed, a table, chair, another door that led to a bathing chamber. The space was simple. Basic. It mattered not besides the fact that it had a large bed and we were alone.

The way she'd responded to the medical probes—after we calmed and reassured her—had been stunning to witness. She was so responsive, not only to the stimulation, but to the strap across her hips, to Ander and his firm grip on her wrists, his spoken commands.

Our mate's pussy had grown wet the moment Ander began issuing orders. Jessica could not hide the truth from us, the truth that she had enjoyed being bound, had grown aroused by the hard strength of Ander's hands on her wrists. Her release had been powerful, her cries echoing through the chamber making my cock hard as a rock, eager to take her, to force her to another peak.

She was too feisty, too headstrong, to give up control. She was a warrior, as we were. But her reaction today had revealed the truth to all three of us: she was indeed stubborn, fierce, and defiant, but she hungered for a mate strong enough to dominate her, a mate with whom she could feel safe enough to let herself go.

I would be that mate. Ander would as well. If she needed to feel our control and dominance when it came to fucking, then we would provide. She wasn't a virgin, but by the surprised look on her face when we'd brought her to climax, any man she'd been with before had not given her what she needed. She'd never before felt safe enough to completely give up control.

The fact that we'd been matched assured me that my conclusions were correct. While I hungered to dominate her, to tease her body and prolong her pleasure until she begged, Ander's stoic power aroused her as well. Ander and I admitted our needs, were comfortable in our roles as her mates, and did not try to hide our darkest desires. The opposite could be said for Jessica. She acted as if her needs were a surprise to her. It became obvious to me, with her chaos of emotions swirling through me via our mating collar, that her mind was at war with her body. Her ego and conditioning compelled her to resist, but her body was incapable of lying. The processing center's matching protocols did not lie. She needed everything we gave her.

That was why my cock was hard as a Prillon pipe and if I didn't fuck her soon I would surely come in my pants. The collars connected us and I sensed not only Jessica's lingering desire but Ander's eagerness as well. The connection we shared was intense, sharp, and hot as hell. I flicked a glance at Ander and he gave me a small nod.

We would take her now. With the collars, there would be no doubt we would be attuned to her every need. If she disliked anything, we would know immediately. Starting now.

"Now that I wear your collar, I'm legally a Prillon bride?" she asked.

"Yes. You belong to us now." I placed her on her feet before us and swiped the blanket from her shoulders, tossing it onto the chair in the corner. She would not need any kind of covering for now. "We will learn all of your secrets, Jessica. You won't be able to hide anything from us."

She shivered but lowered her hands to her sides. She stood before us regal as a queen and my cock swelled to the point of bursting. "I don't understand. I'm not hiding anything now."

Ander tilted his head and raised an eyebrow. "Yes, you are, mate. You're hiding from everyone, including yourself."

A rush of pleasure flooded our connection as Jessica responded to his words, his commanding tone. She licked her lips. "Like what? I'm standing here naked wearing your collar. What could I be hiding?"

"How you like to be fucked," I responded.

Her chin came up with that and I stifled a smile.

"*You* are going tell *me* how I like it?" She arched a brow.

"No," I replied simply. "Your body is going to reveal the secrets you are not willing to admit."

She backed up a step as I continued, "You want us to fuck you hard."

"You want it rough," Ander added. He lifted the hem of his shirt and pulled it up and over his head, dropped it on the floor.

Her eyes fell to Ander's chest and she stared.

"You need to let go, to be told what to do."

"I—no."

"You need to relinquish control when it comes to being fucked by your men," I clarified. "You might be a warrior in your own right, but when you are naked and between the two of us, you will do as we say."

She took another step back, her chest heaving as her arousal climbed. As she turned, I could see the flared end of the plug parting her ass cheeks. My cock pulsed at the sight. Cringing in discomfort, I undid my pants.

"What if I don't? What if you're wrong?" She lifted one hand to rub the top of her chest and side of her neck in a nervous gesture I found utterly endearing. She wanted what we were offering her, but was afraid to take it.

"Do you trust us, Jessica? Do you trust us not to hurt you? Do you believe we are strong enough, disciplined enough, to protect and care for you? Do you believe that our one desire is to make you happy, to meet your needs?"

Her hand froze on the side of her neck and she bowed her head, staring at her feet for several long seconds that felt like a millennium to me, and I was sure, to Ander as well. He held his breath where he stood next to me. We both did, waiting for her answer, waiting for permission to claim her. This one fragile female held our very hearts and happiness in her hands.

I walked to her then, pulling her into my arms so that her ear was pressed to my chest above my beating heart. I held her close, stroking the curve of her back and hip with one hand as Ander watched with an intense need I knew was mirrored in my own gaze. The other hand I tangled in her hair, holding her to me softly, like delicate crystal.

"Do you hear the beating of my heart? It beats for you. Every cell in my body is dedicated to you, to your comfort, to your safety, to your pleasure. The collars around our necks mark you as ours, mate, but in reality, we belong to you. We serve no other but you. We will fight for you, kill for you, die for you. We will do everything in our power to make you feel safe, protected, and loved. If you allow us, Jessica." I cupped her cheek in my hand and tilted her head up so I could look down into her pale blue eyes. "Say yes. Accept our claim. Let us love you."

One word. That's all we needed to make her ours forever. One word would set us free, to touch, to fuck, to mark forever.

"Yes."

I kissed her gently, softly on the lips in acknowledgment of her gift. I did not protest as Ander reached for her hand and gently pulled her away. I knew he, too, was starved for her touch.

I pulled my own shirt from my head and dropped it to the floor as Ander took a hold of Jessica's hand and led her to the bed. "First, dear mate, you will be punished."

"Punished—what? Why?"

He walked alongside the bed, pulling her forward so she had no choice but to crawl up onto the mattress. Only when both her knees were on the soft surface did he release her hand to slide his arm beneath her waist. "Your stubborn refusal to obey Nial earlier caused us to injure two of our brothers and damage the doctor's examination room."

"I said I was sorry about that. I didn't understand." She was on her hands and knees and his free hand caressed her bare bottom as he leaned over to speak in her ear.

"That is not good enough. You put yourself in unnecessary danger, mate, despite the fact that Nial warned you. Did you stop to consider what would have happened had Nial or I lost the challenge?" His hand came down on her bare ass, hard.

Smack!

A pink handprint appeared and she fought to break his hold, but she had no chance of escape. Her face flushed pink as Ander spanked her again. "What the fuck are you doing?"

Ander shook his head. "Language, mate."

He spanked her again. And again.

She panted in his hold, her nipples pebbled into hard peaks and her eyes closed as she fought the arousal I could smell flooding her pussy. "This is stupid. I'm not a child."

"No, you are not. You are mine. You are Nial's. We will pleasure you. We will care for you. And when danger is near, we will protect you." *Smack. Smack.* "If you defy us and place yourself in danger, we will punish you. We will hold you down and spank your bare bottom until it's bright red and your entire body is on fire."

Blinding sensual hunger flooded my collar as Ander spoke to her. I dropped my pants and fisted my hard cock in my hand as I watched him dominate her. She bit her lip and moaned, her breasts swaying under her with each firm strike of Ander's hand on her round ass.

The perfect flesh turned swiftly changed color as his palm struck a different spot each time. I could not deny the fascination with the way her lush ass quivered.

"Ander!"

My second spanked her until she dropped her head, her pussy so wet I could see the glistening call of her arousal from several feet away. Ander struck her once more, hard, then plunged two fingers into her pussy from behind.

"You like a little pain, Jessica? Do you want me to spank you some more?" He pulled his fingers from her pussy and they were shiny and wet when he pushed them in deeper, rubbing her clit with his thumb. "You want me to spank you harder?"

She shook her head, but we all knew differently. Ander groaned and fucked her with his fingers, plunging hard and deep as Jessica's lust flooded both of our collars. I walked to her side and stroked the long, elegant curve of her waist, my eye on the plug in her ass. I leaned down to her other ear. "Do you want us to fuck you with the plug in place? Do you want us to stretch you until it hurts so good and make you scream?"

"Oh, God. I can't. I can't." She whimpered the words, shaking her head side to side as I took over and swatted her ass myself, enjoying the sharp bite of her pain through the collar and the flood of heat that followed behind as I spanked her. She loved being spanked. Loved what Ander was doing to her now, as he used three fingers to spread her pussy wide and the other to tug and play with the plug in her ass.

He did not remove it, but pushed and pulled enough to stretch her pussy and her ass, to make her burn as he finger-fucked her wet core. A sheen of sweat broke out on her skin, her fingers clenching the sheet.

"You forget. The collars connect us all. You cannot lie to us," I told her. "I can feel your struggle, the ache inside as you try to understand how it's possible to find pleasure in the pain."

I spanked her again, the cracking noise of the contact filling the room.

This time, Jessica moaned. "Oh, God."

"I am not a god, but you may call me master." I stepped closer and cupped one full breast in my hand, pinching the nipple, tugging as I smacked her ass again.

"Your pussy never lies. The collars never lie. Surrender, Jessica, do not question your needs, simply accept them and we will pleasure you in ways you've never imagined but always wanted. I bet you never knew having your ass filled would feel so good. There is no shame in giving your desires to your mates to fulfill."

Ander lowered his head and softly nipped at her red ass

with his teeth, just hard enough to make her squirm as I pulled on her breast. We would not relent until she admitted the truth. We felt it through the collar, she felt it in every cell of her being, but she had to accept it. Finally, I saw her shoulders slump, her fingers loosen, her head drop. She gave in, gave over to our mastery of her body, to her needs. To the truth.

"Yes, master," she gasped.

"Do you want us to fuck you?" Ander asked.

She whimpered when he pulled his fingers free and walked to offer them to her. "Open your mouth, taste perfection."

She did, and he slipped the tips of two fingers between her lips. As the taste flooded her body with need, I slipped one finger of my own into her core and removed it to have her taste on my tongue. She was sweet and warm and I could feel my cock weep with the need to plunge deep.

Stepping back, I shed the remainder of my clothes, all the while staring at her exposed pussy, open and eager, swollen and wet. I couldn't deny the gorgeous sight with the plug just above in her ass. With her cheeks red and hot from her spanking, I couldn't want anything more. I ached to get my seed in her, to coat her pussy walls with my essence, to bind us together even further. Just the taste of her on my tongue dragged me under. I belonged to her, utterly and completely. No other woman would ever satisfy me. She owned me and it was time to take extend our bond.

"I'm going to fuck you now. I'm going to put my big cock in this eager pussy."

Jessica's head arched back as Ander forced her head up with a hand around her neck. Her back curved beautifully, her ass high in the air and her legs spread wide as she wiggled her hips in welcome.

"Ander is going to fuck that mouth of yours. It gets you in trouble, mate, and so he's going to keep it occupied."

Ander stripped, too, so we were ready for her. She lifted her head then and her eyes widened as she saw his cock for the first time. It was long and thick, the head of it broad, perhaps too broad for her mouth. She'd take it though; she'd take all of it. I could sense it, could feel her eagerness for it to touch the back of her throat.

A pearly drop of essence dripped from the tip.

"Lick it." Ander stepped close, placing one knee on the bed so his cock bumped her mouth. She had no choice but to open, to flick her tongue over it.

I almost came watching that little pink tongue swipe the fluid away. She groaned and closed her eyes in bliss as the bonding essence in his seed flooded her senses. I watched, awed, as her open pussy clenched down on empty air, eager for me.

I could wait no longer. Stepping up to her, I grabbed hold of the base of my cock, aligned it with her eager entrance. With one hand on her hip, I watched as I pushed forward and my cock disappeared inside her inch by inch. I pulled on her buttocks, spreading her wider and her pussy lips flared open around my thick shaft, the soft pink tissue stretching and opening to take me deep.

Splaying my hand wide, I placed my palm over her perfect ass cheek, and settled my thumb on the base of the plug in her ass, moving the trainer in and out of her body, adding to her sensations. I knew, through the collar about my neck, that while she was adjusting to being filled, she loved it. She was not in pain, but in the most intense pleasure.

Pushing forward, I buried myself to the balls, until she couldn't take any more and I settled there, watching as she eagerly licked the head of Ander's cock, each drop of pre-cum adding to her arousal causing her pussy to clench down on my cock like a fist.

With my free hand, I reached forward and took hold of her long hair, tangling the silken strands around my fingers. As I pulled gently, her head came back so she was in the perfect position to take Ander. Deep.

"Open up, mate, and take us both," Ander nudged

forward so the tip of his cock went into her mouth, forcing her lips apart.

She opened readily, taking the crown of Ander's cock. There was no doubt she was eager for more of the bonding essence to coat her tongue.

"Do you want us to fuck you now?" Ander cupped Jessica's chin as she looked up at him. She made a noise of assent, but she couldn't speak around his meaty cock.

"You'll take us both, mate. Now."

CHAPTER TWELVE

Nial

Ander's order caused Jessica's eyelids to flutter closed and she pushed back against me, trying to force me to move, to fuck her harder.

Ander denied her as well, holding still as he spoke. "I'm going to fuck your throat as Nial fucks that hot, wet pussy."

On cue, I slid out of her core, back in, thrusting deep so that I bumped the tip of her womb. I wanted to come inside her, drown her in my seed, and plant my child deep in her body. But we were not finished with her, not yet. I let Ander talk to her, let him lead her where we wanted her to go. He knew what she needed, knew how to shut off her mind to only his voice, his commands, her pleasure.

He thrust his hips forward as I did the same, fucking her in unison, plunging in and out of her together.

"That's not deep enough, Jessica. Open up. Take us. Swallow me down. Give me more."

Leaning forward, she took more of him as we both plunged deep, trapping her between our hard cocks.

"Good girl. Now, Nial's going to fuck you harder with his big cock. You want his cock, don't you?"

I grabbed her by the hips, my fingers digging into her soft flesh as I fucked her harder and faster as he continued to talk to her. Crude words. Dark words. She loved it. The sound of her wet pussy filled the room. Every time I bottomed out, I forced her body to shift forward, pushing Ander's cock deeper into her mouth. She could not escape us, could not retreat from either of our huge cocks as we fucked her, filled her. Each time I entered, she groaned, making Ander groan, the veins in his neck bulging as he fought to maintain control.

I understood his problem well. The swirling pleasure built, each of our collars adding to the sensations, the pleasure taking us all up, higher and higher.

"He's deep, isn't he, mate? You want your prince to move the plug in your ass? You want him to fuck you with it, too? You want us to fuck all three of your holes?"

He pulled out completely and she licked her lips, looking up at him with glazed eyes. "Yes."

"Yes, master."

"Yes, master. Please. Please. Yes. Please." Her voice was hoarse, thick with desire and desperation. She was no longer thinking, she was ours, totally and completely ours in this moment. Her body was her entire universe, our cocks and our control her only anchor to reality. I loved seeing her like this, lost and eager and totally free.

Ander rubbed her bottom lip with his thumb as he fisted his cock in front of her, stroking it hard and fast so that a large drop of pre-cum gathered on the tip. She watched, almost mesmerized as he leaned forward and rubbed the bonding essence onto her lips. I bit back a growl as her pussy closed around my cock like a vise. I grabbed the end of the butt plug and pulled it back just enough to watch that sweet, round entrance stretch and begin to open, but not hard enough to pull the plug free.

I pushed it back into her body and she gasped as Ander issued his next order. "Then take my cock, mate. Take it all."

Jessica opened her mouth and took him in, her cheeks hollowing out as she stretched her jaw to accommodate his size. He fisted her hair on either side of her face and I let go of my hold in the golden strands so he could force her obedience. "Fill that throat of yours and let me fuck it. Yes, good. More. Oh, you're very good at this. Deeper. *Yes.*"

When Jessica's nose nudged the light-colored curls at the base of his cock, I pulled back then thrust deep, fucking her hard. It pushed her forward so Ander's cock filled her mouth entirely.

Ander pulled back so she could catch her breath and I pulled back as well. She whimpered, feeling empty—the collar link telling us what she could not, making us hyper-aware of her needs—and I thrust into her again. I began to fuck her in earnest, filling her up and pushing her onto Ander's cock. I took her as she took Ander. She was between us, giving everything of herself.

"You love this. You love being told what to do. You love being between your two men. Giving all of yourself. Ah, see, Nial's going to play with your ass, too. To fuck it with that plug." Ander gritted out the last as the pleasure that came from Jessica was like a surge of dark power through our bodies.

"You're not in charge, mate. You won't be in charge when we fuck you. Why? Because it's just what you need. We know what you want, what you need. We know everything about your desires."

Ander kept talking as we took her. She kept her eyes on his as he spoke, as he brushed her hair back from her face as she continued to take him down her throat.

"How do we know that you like it dark and dirty and rough? Because you're matched to us. It's a perfect match. *We're* a perfect match. You will come when I command," Ander told her and she whimpered.

She was so close, so eager for her release. I wasn't going to hold out much longer, the hot, slick feel of her my undoing. I was content allowing Ander to set our pace for now. He pleased our mate with his dirty talk and harsh commands and I was free to simply enjoy our mate's body. For years, as prince, I had been in charge, making decisions that affected millions of lives. For once, I was simply a man, free to give my complete attention to my mate, to feel her wet pussy on my cock, the pleasure that shivered down her spine as I tugged on the butt plug and Ander fucked her mouth. I was free, and fucking the only woman in the universe who mattered to me. Her body was home, now. This intense pleasure, all *mine*.

That one word filled my mind like a primal chant as I plunged my cock in and out of her pussy. *Mine. Mine. Mine.*

I spanked her ass, hard, and she whimpered around Ander's cock, her own hand drifting beneath her body to stroke her clit. I knew any moment her release would grip me in a firestorm of pleasure-pain I would not be able to resist.

I was going to come.

And then, I was going to fuck her again.

• • • • • • •

Jessica

Oh, my God.

I wasn't sure when it had happened, but I was lost between my men. For the second time, completely mindless, as only these two seemed to be able to make me. I had no idea when I'd lost control of my body, when I'd lost the ability to reason. Nor did I care.

I didn't want to think anymore. I wanted to fuck. I wanted to feel like I totally and completely belonged to someone. I was tired of feeling lonely and isolated. I was so tired of facing the world alone. I had no more barriers, no will to resist.

None. I simply floated, flooded with intense satisfaction as I drove my mates harder and faster down my throat and in my pussy. Their attention was laser focused, their naughty words and hard cocks pushing me closer and closer to the edge as I reveled in being what they needed me to be. They needed me wild and eager, they needed me to welcome them, to want their hands and mouths, their cocks and their adoration. I wanted it all, and they were giving it to me, pushing me until my legs trembled and my heart threatened to burst. My ass still stung where they'd spanked me, but even that had just turned me on, the hot sting spreading like a wildfire through my veins. I was on the razor's edge, and they held me there, on the precipice of an explosive orgasm, not letting me go over, forcing my anticipation to build.

I looked up at my second, Ander, as I deep-throated his huge cock. The taste of his seed was like a drug and I couldn't get enough. At first, I hadn't been able to breathe and I'd panicked slightly, but he'd kept his hand on my chin and his eyes on mine. Somehow, I knew he wouldn't hurt me, would push my limits but never place me in danger. I gave him my life in that moment, trusting him to let me take a breath, trusting him to keep me safe as I pleasured him.

Once I felt that reassurance, I'd given over to pleasing him, to fucking him with my mouth. He tasted perfect, manly and dark and the hot feel of his cock, pulsing and thick, made me wetter and wetter.

Ander pulled on my hair and I looked up at him, eager to fulfill his desire, to be whatever he needed me to be. He pulled back and wrapped his own fist around the base of his cock. "Suck on the head, mate. Suck it like it's the best thing you've ever tasted. Suck on it like if you don't swallow me whole you'll die."

I grinned and opened my mouth, pulling the tip of him in and exploring the edges with my tongue as he continued, "If you can't make me come in the next minute, Nial is going to stop fucking you. He's going to pull out of that pussy and leave you empty."

While Ander seemed to be the one in charge, Nial's cock bottomed out inside me and I felt safe in his protective silence. He was the mountain at my back, my anchor as Ander was my storm. In this room, and with the Prillon people, Nial had ultimate power, the power of a prince. But if disobeying Ander would cost me the pleasure of Nial's cock moving deep inside me, I'd do whatever Ander said.

I sucked on him, hard, making him buck and moan until his hand shook as he tried to maintain control. I couldn't allow that. I needed him to lose himself in me with the same mindless pleasure they'd given me. I wanted him to come in my mouth. I wanted to swallow him down and make sure he knew exactly who he belonged to.

What did that make me? A woman eagerly obeying a man's orders? I'd fought my entire life against this level of submission, but here I was, being fucked by two men like a porn star. I should feel debased, dirty even, from Ander's words. But I didn't. I felt powerful locked between them, like a queen holding court with two men so engrossed, so hypnotized by my body, by my mouth and my pussy, by my surrender, that they were losing control.

It was fucking hot. I loved the dirty talk, the taboo way they possessed me together. I was between them, practically skewered by two cocks. I couldn't go anywhere if I tried, and hell, I didn't want to try at all. I wanted to own them both. I wanted them unable to look at me without remembering me like this, without wanting more.

Nial took hold of the plug's base and began to move it in and out of me just as if it were a cock. I was so full. I had every hole filled and fucked and stretched.

I didn't close my eyes, didn't turn my gaze from Ander's. I watched him as I sucked harder, focused on him, obeyed him. I needed him to know I was his, that I wanted him in my body more than I wanted to breathe.

I *needed* to obey him more than I needed to come.

"I can't hold out any longer," Nial growled as his hips slapped against my ass, pushing that plug in deep.

"Jessica," Ander growled and I pulsed my tongue against the tip of his cock and squeezed down as hard as I could on

Nial's cock in my pussy. Nial groaned and I did it again as Ander gave us all what we wanted.

"Count three thrusts of Nial's cock, mate, and then come."

That permission winged through my body like a jolt of electricity and I held off my orgasm by a sheer force of will, my eyes drifting closed as Nial plunged deep.

One.

Ander's cock swelled in my mouth.

Two.

Nial's fingers on my hip tightened, his palm gripping flesh that still tingled from the spanking.

Three.

Nial slammed hard against me, filling me completely. When I felt the hot jet of his seed filling me, I came.

Ander groaned as he let go of his cock and pushed deep once more, hitting the back of my throat as the pulsing of his own seed slid straight down, warming me like a shot of whiskey.

Their seed filled me and I lost my balance as wave after wave of pleasure coursed over me, my nipples tightening, my inner walls clenching around both Nial's cock and the plug in my ass. I tasted Ander's tangy flavor on my tongue as the hot wash of their essence seeped into me, lulling me and almost drugging me with the hottest, sweetest pleasure.

Ander pulled back, letting me catch my breath as Nial pulled his cock from me. Gently, he slipped the plug out as he worked my clit with two fingers and my body was so primed and ready I came again as he pulled the plug, stretching me wide and squeezing my clit.

Both men left me then, all at once I was empty. I collapsed onto my side on the bed, the unique tang of Ander's seed on my tongue and Nial's dripping from my pussy and onto my thighs.

I couldn't catch my breath, couldn't move, even if I wanted to.

As I fought for air, I glanced up at my men. Their cocks

were still hard, both red and shiny, glistening with my arousal, my saliva, and their seed. They stood shoulder to shoulder watching me.

"You're not done, mate." Ander's words slipped under my skin and my nipples were instantly hard, my empty pussy aching. They looked sated, their expressions less intense, but their cocks had not deflated in the slightest. Were they truly ready to go again?

"You're going to take my ass now?" I asked him.

He shook his head. "You're not ready. Soon."

"My… my pussy then?"

Nial spoke. "Your pussy is mine until you are bred. My seed must fill you and take root. As your primary mate, your first child is, by rights, mine. Once you are carrying my child, we will share that sweet pussy. Until then, and after you are well trained, he will take your ass."

"Then—" I frowned. "What do you want now?" I'd already given them everything.

"I can feel your desire. It is not quenched," Ander said.

It was true. I should be exhausted or unconscious, at the very least sore. I was none of those things. In fact, I was achy and desperate for more. "How—"

"You forget, mate, we know your needs," Nial said. He'd allowed Ander to issue the orders up until now, but his tense facial expression made me believe that was about to change. "Part those thighs and show me your pussy."

I should have been appalled by Nial's command, but I could do nothing but obey. They'd only brought me pleasure so there was no reason to question. Besides, I'd just fucked both of them, so the time for modesty had passed.

Slowly, I shifted to lie on my back so I could part my legs. I bent my knees and let them fall open so he could see all of me.

"Now, show me how you touch yourself."

Nial knelt at the foot of the bed and took one ankle. Ander copied him and took the other so they were *right there* seeing *everything*. There was no way they could miss my swollen folds. Or the seed that now coated my fingers. Or my clit that was huge and pulsing. Or my entrance that was clenching with eagerness for more cock. Or my back entrance, probably red and softened from the plug and rough use.

"Spread my seed all over that perfect pussy," Nial commanded.

I did as he said and I could feel the hot slide of it warm me, soothe me, and make me so hot. It *was* an aphrodisiac. It was like C-bomb. I'd been drugged by my men's desires.

"Oh, my God," I moaned, circling my clit with Nial's seed.

"Lick your fingers," he said.

I lifted them to my mouth and sucked on them as Nial knelt between my legs and pushed his cock deep.

The taste of Nial's seed overlaid Ander's flavor and Nial's powerful frame was on top of me even as his huge cock spread me wide. Ander moved, climbing on the bed until he knelt above my head. He leaned forward and reached over the top of me to push my knees wider as Nial fucked me. I lowered my hands to fist the sheets, but Ander grabbed them and lifted them over my head, placing them on his cock.

"Suck my balls as he fucks you, mate. Pump my cock in your hands and suck on my balls until he makes you come."

Oh, God! He was so fucking naughty, such a bad, bad boy. I bucked my hips off the bed, wrapped my ankles around Nial's hips, whimpering and begging him not to stop fucking me with each second of air I could spare. I worked Ander's cock with my hands, twisting and fisting him, so attuned to him through the collar that I knew exactly what he liked.

When I lost my breath, I sucked in another one, begging Nial to fuck me faster, to strike my clit, to touch me.

As the crescendo built in our bodies, the collar's feedback loop fed my mind data. The way Nial's cock felt as he fucked me. The tight joy of my hands around Ander's cock. Their satisfaction and pleasure as I arched and moaned, begging them to hurry, to make me scream.

Nial braced himself and slid one hand between us to stroke my clit as Ander stroked and plucked my breasts. I sucked him and felt him lose control, felt the hot jets of his seed as the warm liquid landed all over my breasts. He massaged it into my skin, the bonding essence making me scream as release after release rocked through me.

Nial fucked me until I couldn't take anymore, until I was numb, and then he buried himself deep and filled me up. I was lost. I was ruined. I was dirty and slutty and totally theirs. I loved it. God, I loved it all.

They laid down beside me, Nial in front of me and Ander at my back as we all collapsed into exhausted, very satisfied heaps on the bed. They both faced me, their hands on me, petting and soothing me, thanking me and letting me know I was special, precious. Theirs.

I'd never felt so complete, so content in my life.

I didn't know how long they stroked me in tender silence, but when a loud beep sounded, I jumped like a startled rabbit.

I heard a beep, then another one, then a man's voice. "My apologies, Prince Nial. An urgent message arrived for you."

"Speak," Nial called loudly.

I looked at his face and lifted my hand to trace the sharp angles of his cheek and brow. I stroked the soft, silver skin left by his enemies and allowed my gaze, and my fingertips, to travel farther down his body, over the silver section of his shoulder and down his arm to his hand. He caught mine in his and lifted it to his lips, bestowing a kiss on my palm as we listened to the messenger speak through the communication system. I tried not to cringe as I realized I'd screamed loud enough when I'd come all those times. Surely, every man in the Colony knew what my men had been doing to me just a few minutes ago. Had they been listening outside the door, waiting to activate the message system after we were done?

The thought was mortifying, but I shoved that emotion away. I wouldn't trade what just happened for anything. Hell, if I had to let a roomful of strangers watch to experience that pleasure again, I would. No question.

"We have urgent news, Prince Nial. If you could come to the command room when it's... convenient, we can update you."

"Are we in immediate danger?" Nial asked and I felt Ander tense beside me, his hand on my hip gone suddenly still.

"No, prince. If you'll come to the—"

"Tell me now," Nial commanded.

"Very well," the voice replied. "It's the Prime. Your father has been killed. His transport was attacked by the Hive on the front. There were no survivors."

I watched as Nial's eyes closed a bit too hard, his mouth thin as he clenched his jaw. Ander squeezed my hip, as if in reassurance, but I was not afraid. I was worried at the pain and regret I could feel through my connection with Nial.

"Thank you for the news. Is that all?" Nial asked.

"No. The Prillon high council has declared there will be a Death Match for the right of ascension."

Ander cursed and Nial opened his eyes with a look that would have made me shiver with fear if it had been directed at me. "When?"

"Tomorrow at dusk."

"Of course." Nial looked at me then, our gazes locking as I tried to tell him with my eyes that I was his, that I was on his side no matter what happened. "Have my father's transport bans been lifted?"

"Yes. We can transport you to the home world whenever you are ready."

"We'll be ready shortly."

"Um, sir, there was one other thing."

Nial frowned. "Yes?"

"The doctor asked me to remind the princess of her

promise to make contact with the Lady Egara on Earth. Word of possible brides has spread and is causing a disturbance among the warriors."

He looked down at me, a question in his eyes. I smiled and nodded. Of course. Any human woman who turned down a pair of hotties like mine was just plain crazy.

Nial's grin said he understood exactly why I agreed so readily. "Of course. The princess will make her call prior to our departure tomorrow."

"Thank you, sir. Comm out."

Ander pressed himself to my side and rested his head on my shoulder as he looked at Nial. "Are you going to challenge for the throne?"

Nial nodded. "Yes. But I should not have to. It is mine."

Ander snorted and wrapped an arm around my waist. "Kill them all, Nial. No mercy."

"I have none to give."

I didn't understand everything going on, but I knew what a Death Match usually meant and I felt my eyes tear up with a hundred emotions I could not name as I looked at my mate's face. I would never tell Nial not to fight. That was not the way of the warrior, but I could worry. And I could offer solace when he returned to me, victorious. For he would emerge the victor. He had to.

I cupped his cheek in my hand. "If you have to kill them all, do it quickly, mate. Then come back to me. You're mine now."

He smiled then. "Always."

I nodded and held back my tears. I belonged to my mates now, body and soul, but once I stopped feeling so damn good, I would find out about Nial's father, this stupid death battle for the throne, and figure out a way to help Nial defeat his enemies. He was mine, and no one was taking him from me.

CHAPTER THIRTEEN

Ander

The bright orange glow of the setting stars filled the sky as Nial and I stepped off the transport platform on Prillon Prime, our mate between us, and walked the short distance to the palace arena. Already crowds gathered on the walkways, lining up to enter the arena and witness the duel to come. Many looked upon us with terror as we passed, some with curiosity, but none with welcome. Nial and I were both taller than most males on the planet. Our size, armor, and altered features were enough to send more than one male scrambling to get out of our way.

"It's this way." Nial led us down a side corridor and I followed, keeping our mate safely between us.

"It's beautiful here." Jessica wore a long gown of dark red, the color of house Deston, of the royal house. The collar around her neck would remain black until the claiming ceremony, but Nial had wanted everyone to know exactly whom she belonged to and I had agreed. Compared to the plain black and brown armor worn by most warriors, she stood out like a flame in a sea of darkness.

I had only been to the royal palace once before, years

ago when I'd first been scarred and the Prime himself had pinned a medal on my chest and named me a hero.

The only thing I'd done was survive. My entire squad had been lost, but I'd been in the one ship carrying Hive intel back to command. Somehow, I'd maintained control of my ship and lived through the blast. I'd stayed alive. My brothers in arms had died, and the leader of our planet had labeled me a hero.

I'd sworn never to come back to this place again. I hated everything about it: the tall quartz pillars, the incessant chatter of hundreds of servants, and the wide-eyed, frightened looks of the civilians who looked upon a warrior in armor and chased after him with stars in their eyes.

Warriors were like prime steaks on display at a meat market here on the planet's surface. If we survived the wars, we were considered the best mates, the strongest and most dangerous of our people. And they were right. If anyone so much as sneered at Jessica, I would remove their head from their body and stomp on the remains. This possessiveness was new, and pure instinct. My mate had shocked me with her lust, her acceptance, and her desire to please. She'd given us everything, submitted completely, which should have made me feel like I had mastered her. Instead, I simply felt humbled by her acceptance of my scars, my needs. All of me. I felt loved, and for the first time in my life I actually knew what that word meant.

I loved Jessica. And now, something threatened to tear our new family apart. I had offered myself as Nial's second on a whim, fully expecting him to refuse. That had been the best decision I'd ever made. That moment brought me to Jessica, and I was not willing to give her up. Losing Nial would destroy her. She was attached to us both, but it had not escaped my notice than when she needed to be pushed, to be wild and out of control, she turned to me. When the world got too big for her and she needed to feel safe, it was Nial whose touch she sought, Nial whose promises she trusted.

She needed us both, and I would not see her suffer.

Nial navigated the back corridors and secret doorways with ease and I was grateful we did not need to attempt to force our way through the throngs of spectators above. When we reached the very edge of the arena floor, Nial spoke to a guard, who would lead Jessica and myself to a designated seating area, and Nial into the arena.

Jessica flung herself into Nial's arms and kissed him with a passion that made my cock hard, despite the situation. She was fire in his arms, and she was clearly marking him as her own. "Kill them all, then come back to me. Don't forget who you belong to now. You're mine, my prince."

Nial nodded, but did not speak, and I led Jessica away following a guard in black armor to a pair of seats near the center of the arena. We were in the very front row, a waist high wall of stone all that would separate Jessica from the battles below.

We sat just as a loud boom rattled the seats and everyone hushed in a strange silence, waiting to hear the announcement of who entered the arena next.

"Prince Nial Deston." The voice boomed from somewhere, and pandemonium broke out. People cheered. People booed. Arguments began in the seats with everyone pushing and shoving at those around them trying to get a better look at the prince, the contaminated prince and his silver eye.

Jessica grabbed my hand and I held her with the other on my weapon as Nial walked to the center of the arena below us. Opposite him, seven large warriors stood in line, presenting themselves to the Prillon high council.

At the mention of Prince Nial's name, four of the challengers turned immediately and walked out of the arena. Jessica leaned forward to watch one of them disappear down a side tunnel. "Where are they going?"

I wasn't a politician, but I knew well enough what had happened. "They don't want to challenge if there is a legitimate heir to the throne. They've declined."

"Oh, thank God! That only leaves three." She seemed so pleased that I didn't argue. Three or seven, it would make no difference, not to Nial.

As I watched Nial step forward, he bowed to the high council and staked his claim to the throne.

"I am Prince Nial Deston, son of Prime Deston, rightful heir to the throne of Prillon."

One of the elders leaned over the short wall separating them from the arena opposite us and shook his finger in Nial's direction. "You were disowned, Nial. Everyone knows you are contaminated and fit for neither a bride nor the crown."

Nial held his head high and I stood, pulling Jessica to her feet beside me. Nial lifted his hand and pointed in our direction. "May I present my bride and my second, Jessica Smith of Earth, and Ander, legendary warrior of the battleship *Deston*."

Silence thick enough to slice settled over the gathered crowd as they tried to make sense of Nial's words. No contaminated warrior had ever returned to Prillon, let alone with a bride and second. It was unheard of.

Two of the challengers bowed low to Jessica and walked from the arena, also declining their attempt at the throne, leaving just one warrior facing Nial.

The council member who had spoken the first time addressed Nial again. "As the only challenger, we name Commander Vertock Prime, Nial Deston. What say you to that?" Nial's name was no more than a sneer.

"I issue a warrior's challenge, as is my right. I challenge Prime Vertock to a Death Match for the throne of Prillon Prime." Nial turned to face his opponent and the entire crowd settled into their seats, eager to see the fight. All but Jessica.

She stood tall, a symbol of Nial's legitimacy, her squared shoulders and the proud tilt of her chin daring any to challenge her mate's worth. I sensed her fear, her worry, but it did not show to anyone who looked upon her. If I hadn't loved her before, I would have fallen in love with her in this moment.

Reluctantly, I tore my gaze from my beautiful mate to scan the crowd and watch for danger. I could not spare eyes for Nial's fight. That he would have to win on his own to settle the conditions of the duel. My role was to keep Jessica safe in this sea of potential danger.

Only one of the warriors now circling each other would survive, and Jessica needed it to be Nial.

A soft bell sounded and the opponent charged at Nial, trying to take him to the ground. Nial sidestepped easily, wrapped his arms around the man's neck as he passed and gave one brutal, merciless twist.

The sound of breaking bone filled the arena.

That was it, just as I'd expected. It wasn't a fight. It wasn't a *duel*. It was just death and it had come with a simple twist of Nial's hands. There was no opponent for him, no equal in the crowd. Perhaps I could offer a true test of his strength, but I did not wish to challenge him.

The crowd erupted into loud screams of encouragement or denial, depending on who they backed for victory. When silence reigned once more, Nial dropped the dead challenger to the sandy ground and lifted his arms above his head.

"Is there no other who wishes to die today?"

When no one stepped forward, the crowd settled immediately, but the high council members were all on their feet, seven old, stooped creatures with scowls on their faces. Their speaker had hands on his hips and glared at Nial.

"You cannot be our Prime, even after that victory. You are contaminated."

Nial stepped forward. "What, exactly, does that mean?" He pointed to his face. "I have the marks of a warrior. The Hive implants are obvious signs that I fought the enemy and survived. I stood before you, *contaminated*, as you call it, and defeated the only challenger in this entire arena. I defeated him with a flick of my wrist and you dare name me unworthy? Do you issue challenge yourself, councilor? If so, I will accept."

The old man flubbed his speech, but his eyes spewed hatred. "You are not worthy, Nial."

"Because I am a veteran?" I knew Nial used the Earth word intentionally and I felt Jessica's pride flare. "Because I protected the Prillon people as a warrior and would now do so as their leader?"

Nial lifted his hands and turned to address the crowd. "Do I appear weak or contaminated, Prillon people? I know the enemy. Survived the enemy. I survived my battle with the Hive. I live now with the experience and knowledge to protect this planet. To lead it to ultimate victory."

The old man sputtered, clearly having no retort, and sat back down in his chair as the crowd cheered. There may have been some who disagreed, but the crowd was pleased with Nial, satisfied with his proof of strength and leadership. And with his beautiful Earthen bride. Warriors who had earned the right to claim a bride were well regarded. Those lucky enough to be accepted by their chosen mate, judged worthy by their bride, even more so. And Jessica, with her proud stance and eyes only for her mate, made it very clear that she not only accepted Nial as her mate, but cared for him as well.

Jessica let go of my hand, and before I could stop her she was racing down the stairs and out the lower door onto the arena floor. I leapt over the low stone wall to land in the soft sand and followed her, ensuring no one would dare harm her. Nial would protect her and so would I.

She ran, her dress like a liquid flame behind her, and threw herself in Nial's arms as the crowd roared. I watched it all with a grin. That was my mate, my family, and they were safe for another day.

And I didn't even have to kill anyone to keep it that way.

I thought everything was fine, until two men dragged the dead body away and Nial stood alone in the center of the arena as the chanting began.

"Claiming! Claiming! Claiming!"

The crowd was not leaving, and Jessica's devotion to Nial worked against us as she clung to him for all to see.

Two hundred years ago, when the first Deston ruler challenged for the throne and won, he and his second had fucked his queen on the arena floor, claiming her for all to see.

Tradition demanded Nial and I claim Jessica here and now, in front of the whole world, for those not seated here watched from home, or on the view screens aboard their battleships in deep space as the duel had been broadcast live across the planet and to all known battle groups in space.

Nial had just killed a man in front of billions. And now his people wanted to see the grand finale.

CHAPTER FOURTEEN

Jessica

I threw myself into Nial's arms and he lifted me off my feet for a kiss. I could hear the crowd cheer at the bold sight. I felt all of his adrenaline, all of his power flow through the collars and into the kiss.

When he placed me back on my feet, he stroked my hair back from my face. "You feared for me, mate?"

I shook my head and looked into his one golden, one silver eye. "Never."

"Good girl," he replied.

I felt Ander at my back, my men surrounding me. I did not worry for the crowd, for I knew the two of them would defend me from every single one of them. I was safe. Nial was safe. We were together. But not quite…

Claiming. Claiming. Claiming. The chant filled the air and a look I knew well settled deep in Nial's eyes. Lust. Love. Desire. It was all there.

"I must be claimed," I said. It wasn't a question.

Ander slid my hair over my shoulder and he lowered his head to kiss my neck and then lower still to my collar as Nial spoke.

"We are connected by the collars, but the bond is not complete. We must both fuck you. Together." I saw the need on Nial's face, felt it through the collar, but I sensed also the seriousness behind this requirement.

"Right now?"

"Yes, mate. Right now, in this arena. In front of the entire world."

Holy shit. I turned in his arms, scanning the faces in the crowd. They were not looking upon us with glee or malice, but with a seriousness that made my knees feel weak. "Why?"

Ander spoke from behind me. "In a normal claiming ceremony, the primary mate chooses his closest brothers to bear witness to the act and swear allegiance and protection to his bride."

I bit my lip, remembering the chanting I'd heard during the processing center's simulation. The male voices surrounding me and their chorus of *May the gods witness and protect you.*

Nial lifted his hand to my cheek, holding my gaze when I felt like running. "I am now Prime. King of this world. The entire planet honors and respects our family above all others. They all wish the honor of bearing witness to your claiming, of swearing their oath to serve and protect you."

"Oh, God." I leaned into his hand and tried to remember to breathe. This wasn't just fucking for pleasure. It was a sacred act, a bonding that joined me to both Nial and Ander permanently, in front of a billion witnesses.

This was what it meant to be a queen on Prillon. I thought back to my idea of being a princess, to fancy dresses and high-heeled shoes, to ballroom dancing with a perfect, handsome prince. This was nothing like that fantasy. This was me and my mates, raw and dirty and fucking on the ground in front of the entire planet.

I imagined the people's faces as they watched us fuck, imagined them running home as quickly as possible to alleviate their own needs. I imagined the women closing their eyes with pleasure as they heard my screams, and the men, the warriors in the crowd admiring my body and my breasts, envying my mates as they filled me. The idea made my pulse race and my pussy grow wet.

Maybe I was meant to be the queen of Prillon after all.

Once Nial and Ander claimed me, once my collar changed color to match their deep, royal red, there would be no question, no doubt in anyone's mind that we were the royal family, that Nial was mine, that Ander was mine. And I belonged to them.

That would only occur when they both fucked me at the same time. A wave of desire coursed through me at the thought of them taking me in such a way.

"She is pleased with the idea," Ander murmured against my neck.

"Jessica, this is a public claiming. We must do it here, in front of everyone. There will be no privacy, for I am their new leader and my bonding ceremony must not be questioned. It is the right of all Prillon citizens to witness it, for you and Ander will be their rulers, a part of me, and they must know and trust that all three of us are worthy. Worthy to lead the planet." Nial's words were clear. He wanted me to know now what his people, *our people*, wanted.

"It is not law," Ander added, his tongue flicking over the pulse at my neck. "Nial can refuse if you do not wish to do this."

"But?" I said, knowing there was more.

"But the people will judge him soft, weak, too weak to master his bride."

I shook my head. What the men had done for me made me want to give them everything in return. I was the link that connected them. I was the link that made them strong. That made *us* strong. If I had to fuck them in front of an audience—a very, very large one—it did not matter. I would not weaken Nial as a leader by refusing him this.

Let them watch. Let them envy me. I was giving myself to Nial and Ander. No one else. I was proud of my men.

Proud to share with all Prillon people that I was the one they wanted, the one they desired, the one to make their cocks hard. It was my privilege to be theirs and I was willing to prove that to the entire galaxy.

"I understand. I will do as you wish," I replied.

Ander turned me so they were both in front of me. I looked up at my men. One dark, one fair. One a powerful leader, one a powerful commander. I would submit to them both because my body needed it. My mind needed it.

I was theirs. I knew it. It was time they did, too.

"Are you sure, mate?"

I offered them a smile, let my acceptance flow through me so they could sense my contentment and peace with the decision through our collars. "When you fuck me together, it will bond us permanently?"

Nial nodded. "Your collar will turn red and our claim will be permanent."

"Do you want this? Do you want to fuck me together? Now? In front of everyone?"

"Gods, yes." Ander's body nearly shook as he lowered his chin to look at me. I turned my gaze back to Nial.

"I don't doubt our match, do you?"

"Never," Nial swore. "This would be for the people of Prillon and you shall be their queen."

"Then I will give my people what is expected and I will give my men what they need."

I felt their desire pulse and I grabbed their hands. Warm and strong. Powerful.

"You will not be in control," Ander said. "You must submit to us."

I felt my nipples pebble at his words.

Nial took hold of my chin. "While you are a fierce warrior, it must be shown that you choose us, that you find us worthy. You prove our worth when you willingly submit to your mates."

Ander grinned. "I doubt that will be hard for you."

I slowly shook my head at the thought. "No, for I like to

give over to you. I like to let you lead, to be in charge… in bed."

I moaned as the heat of their desires flooded me through the collars. It wasn't fair, really. They only had to deal with my emotions, my lust. I was flooded with the needs and wants of two powerful warriors.

"There is no bed here, Jessica, but we will be your masters."

Nial lifted his armored shirt off over his head, baring his massive chest and shoulders to the crowd, to me, and the crowd roared as they realized what was about to happen.

"Say it, Jessica."

"You are my masters."

"That's right," Nial replied. His hands came to the front of my gown and he tore it with the strength of a warrior. The filmy fabric shred and fell to a pile at my feet.

The cheering became deafening, an explosion of sound that struck my chest like a punch. I was now naked in an arena full of people. I froze, unsure whether to cover myself, turn, or parade around like a peacock. What was I supposed to do now?

"Eyes on me," Ander commanded and I nearly sighed with relief. My head angled to look at him, to see the stern, yet loving look in his eyes. "You will listen to our voices, feel our need through the collar, do as we say, and you will be pleasured. Nothing else matters. Do you understand, mate?"

"Yes, master."

Nial moved out of sight, but I didn't break eye contact with Ander.

"What are we going to do to you?" he asked.

I licked my lips. "Nial is going to fuck my pussy while you fuck my ass."

No one in the arena could hear our words, but I flushed anyway, the naughty words making me clench my thighs together in anticipation.

Ander took a step closer and put his big hands on my

shoulders. "That's right. You're going to be between us, mate. Connecting us. Bonding the three of us together. While you might feel that we are controlling you, I want you to realize you are the one with the true power."

"Power?" What was he talking about? I had no power here.

"Nial and I are just men without you. Warriors, surely, but nothing more. You are what make us a family. You are what will give us children. You are the one who makes us strong."

"But I submit," I countered.

"By choice. Your submission is a gift and we cherish it."

Ander glanced over my shoulder to something behind me. "It is time."

Before I could respond, he picked me up in his arms and carried me a short distance to where Nial was waiting.

Nial's knuckles stroked down my cheek. "Say the word, Jessica, and we will do this in privacy."

I thought on Ander's words. I held the power. Nial just proved that. I had the final say. I was could tell him I was afraid or ashamed and they'd whisk me away with no further questions. They'd fight the dissenters to make me happy. They'd do anything for me.

So I would do this for them. It was not even a decision, for even though the people could see my naked body, only Nial and Ander could see inside me, could know my thoughts, fears and desires. I let my love for my mates flood me, my eagerness to please them, to make them proud, to honor them in front of their people. I looked into Nial's eyes as I spoke, my voice calm and even. "You can sense the truth through my collar. Let it speak for me. Tell me, masters, what is it saying?"

I felt the flare of pride, of triumph and burning desire return to me through the connection.

Nial's hands lifted to my waist. "It is saying it is time to bond you to your mates. Forever."

"Forever," I repeated.

"Forever," Ander vowed.

In the short time since the duel, a chair had been brought out to the arena floor. Set in the sand was a chair, a throne. It wasn't gilded or fancy, but I knew it was the seat of their leader. It had a tall back and arms and a cushioned seat, but was otherwise unadorned. It was a warrior's chair, not a gilded throne adorned with jewels or gold.

Nial walked to the throne and sat, the leader of his people claiming his rightful place and the crowd roared its approval. He crooked a finger and I responded, walking toward him with my head held high, my shoulders back. I did not try to hide my body. I was not ashamed. I'd never felt more beautiful than I did as the cheering continued, the people urging me on, eager to watch my mates fuck me. My pussy ached for what was to come and I felt the men's eagerness as well. Nial's hard cock was ready and waiting for me. I could see it pressed against his pants.

One step, two, and I was before him. Wrapping a hand about my waist, he pulled me to stand between his parted knees.

"Are you ready for me?" Our eyes were at the same height and I saw the warmth there, the love. The need.

"Why don't you find out?" I asked saucily.

Nial grinned as he placed his hand at the center of my chest, then slid it down my body to cup my pussy, his fingers slipping over the swollen folds, the drenched flesh.

Ander moved behind me and reached around to cup my breasts.

"She's dripping on my hand," Nial said.

My eyes fell closed as they gently touched me, stroking me. I could hear the crowd, but their fervor faded, becoming white noise—there, but not worthy of my notice.

"It's only the three of us, Jessica. No one else matters," Nial said, slipping a finger deep inside my wet heat.

"Yes," I replied, my response less in regards to his statement and more to his invading finger.

"We will fuck you here, for all to see, bond us together

forever," Ander said, his fingers plucking my nipples. "Then we will take you away from here, tie you down, and fuck you again."

"And again," Nial added. "This is only the first of many times we will make our claim today."

Nial's finger slipped from my pussy and I felt empty. A whimper escaped and I opened my eyes to watch as Nial opened his pants and pulled his cock free. I saw the pearly drop of his seed at the tip and I leaned forward to flick it with my tongue.

The crowd roared anew, louder than ever before, and I triumphed because I could feel Nial's surprise and desire through the collar. Ander pulled me up and I met Nial's eyes. He yelled his next question, loud enough for all to hear.

"Do you accept my claim, mate? Do you give yourself to me and my second freely, or do you wish to choose another primary mate?"

Hushed whispers surrounded us and I felt the faintest sliver of tension in both of my men as they waited for my answer. I raised my voice so all would hear me. "I am proud to accept you as my mate, Nial. Proud to accept Ander as my second."

Nial's voice grew impossibly louder. "I claim you in the rite of naming. You are mine and I shall kill any other warrior who dares touch you."

The crowd erupted into cheers and Nial leaned forward so I could hear him over the din. "Straddle me and take me deep. You set the pace, mate."

While they were in charge, this position put me as the dominant. I was the one in control, because they allowed it. I felt giddy with power, with my ability to make my mates hunger for me, ache for me. I wanted them out of control, so overcome with lust they could no longer permit me to torment them. I wanted them desperate and rough.

Putting one knee on either side of Nial's hips, I hovered over his thighs. As he held his turgid cock, I settled lower until the crown pressed against my entrance. Our eyes met, held.

This was it. I dictated when, how fast and how deep. I wanted to make him buck and moan. I wanted to give him all of me, so I lowered myself onto him in one long, smooth stroke.

My head fell back and I groaned as his cock stretched me wide, the sensation of being full only the beginning of what I knew was coming. Nial's hands gripped my hips and held me in place with his cock buried deep. He was all the way in, his cock so big that I felt as if he'd claimed me already. Shifting his hips, Nial slid lower in the chair and I was angled over him slightly, my bottom sticking out.

Ander was right there, waiting. His hand came to my bottom and stroked over it as he leaned forward, placing his other hand on the arm of the chair.

"You're going to feel my fingers on that tight little ass," Ander said. I did and I startled, but I wanted this. I remembered what it felt like when Nial fucked me with the plug in my ass. The sensation so intense that I longed to feel it again. But this time, I knew, would be even more. Ander's cock was huge, and hard, and warm. I wanted his hard body at my back, his arms around me plucking my breasts as they both fucked me. I wanted Nial sliding into my pussy with that look of ecstasy on his face, his strong chest mine to explore, his lips mine to kiss. I wanted his tongue down my throat as they fucked me, as they made me writhe and scream and come so many times I forgot my own name. I moaned, already feeling lost.

"Shh," Ander crooned. "There's lubricant on my fingers. You feel how slick they are. I'm going to work it into you, over you, then on my cock so I'll slide right in."

As he spoke, he began to push and stretch my opening, taking his time to work a finger into me. I kept my eyes on Nial's as Ander worked. Somehow, Nial remained still, content with just his cock filling me. I could sense his eagerness to fuck, to slide out and thrust deep, but he was going to wait so they could take me together.

I sucked in a breath when Ander's finger breached my back entrance. It was then that he began to work the lube into me thoroughly. I didn't know how long it took, but he was liberal with it and his finger was able to slide in easily and without discomfort. I clenched my inner muscles around Nial's cock and wiggled my hips, ready for Ander. I wanted him inside me. I needed both of my mates. I needed to feel taken, owned, claimed. I wanted everyone from this damn planet to know these two men were mine. I owned them. I was the only woman in the universe who could give them such pleasure.

Mine.

Perhaps it was the collars that allowed Ander to sense my response to his touch, for he tended to me perfectly. All at once, he pulled free and I looked over my shoulder to see him pull his cock from his pants and coat it with the lube. It was red and swollen, pulsing and eager, shiny and slick.

Nial took hold of my chin and turned me to face him again.

"Once Ander is in that virgin ass, we'll fuck you."

My eyes widened when I felt Ander's cock poised at my back entrance, then as he nudged forward. I closed my eyes as Ander's dirty talk reached my ears, turning me on.

"Breathe, Jessica. Think of how good it's going to feel. Can you sense Nial's need for you? He's holding back. Your pussy is so hot and tight that it's making him hurt. You're so perfect for us, just being in that hot pussy can make him come." Ander talked as he pushed further. "I'm so hot for you, my cock is aching to get inside. Relax, breathe, feel our need."

I sighed and focused on the collar's power, the connection I shared with my mates. I let their pleasure wash over me. I sighed at the bliss of it and all at once, Ander pushed past that tight ring and he was in.

Crying out, I opened my eyes and looked at Nial.

"That's it. Such a good girl. You're so tight." It was

Nial's turn to reassure me, Ander apparently so overcome by slowing filling my ass with his thick cock that he couldn't speak.

Arching my back, I allowed him to slide even further. There was no pain, only the unbelievable sensation of being filled. I didn't know if they could both fit, but I wanted more. I needed all of them in me. I saw the white-knuckled grip of Ander's hands on the arms of the chair. He used them to anchor himself, to push against as he pushed even deeper. With Nial's hands on my hips, I was not moving, caught—trapped—between them.

Their skin radiated heat; the musky scent of them, of fucking, swirled around us.

I felt Ander's thighs against my bottom and I knew I'd taken all of him.

"Now you are mine, Jessica Smith," Nial whispered against my lips. He lifted me up and dropped me on his cock as Ander slid back and thrust deep.

They began to fuck me then, in and out, alternating their motions. I could do nothing but hold on, my hands going to Nial's tense shoulders.

I wasn't doing anything, just letting them fuck me, to take both my holes in any way they saw fit. In a way they knew I needed.

It wasn't enough. I wanted my fantasy. I wanted it all.

I reached behind me to find Ander's hands. Once I had a hold of his wrists, I lifted them to cup my breasts, my intentions clear. He chuckled, but gave me what I wanted.

Next, I buried my hands in Nial's hair and pulled his head down to mine and claimed his mouth in a kiss. I held back, teasing his tongue forward, asking him without words to kiss me as if he were fucking my mouth.

When I couldn't move, couldn't breathe, when every part of my body felt totally owned, claimed, worshipped by my mates, I let myself drift away, trusting them to give me what I needed. Trusting them to take care of me.

They didn't hurt me, but they weren't gentle. It wasn't

painful, but it was intense. It wasn't sweet or tender, but sweaty, hot, wet fucking.

And I loved it. I was going to come and nothing was going to stop it. I stiffened, my inner muscles clamping down on both of my mates, forcing guttural sounds from both of their throats. "Masters, I... I can't—"

"Come, mate. Come hard and let everyone know you belong to us."

I'd forgotten about the crowd, but Nial's words only forced me over the precipice. I screamed my pleasure as I squeezed their cocks. Everyone could see me coming. They could see how very well my men pleasured me. My mates made me feel cherished and loved, and safe in their arms. They'd broken me into pieces and then made me whole.

I let my head fall back on my shoulders, a huge smile on my face as I ground my hips down and clenched my inner muscles as tightly as I could. The collar around my neck had hummed, then felt warm. I wondered if it had changed color, if when next I looked it would be red, just like my mates'. They were mine forever, and they pleased me well. I was proud the entire planet bore witness to that.

Heat pulsed at my neck, hotter and hotter as I felt Ander thrust hard and fill me with his seed, his essence filling my back passage. Nial groaned and swelled within my pussy. With a tight grip on my hips, I felt him come, his seed jetting into me. I was full, brimming with their mark of ownership, their claim. I was well and completely taken.

I could feel their releases through the collar, feel their pleasure and it made me come again. The collar so hot against my neck, the intensity of the feelings pulsing from it caused tears to form in my eyes, the emotions too much for my human body to hold.

Closing my eyes, I collapsed in their arms. The men's deep breaths were the only things I could hear. Their cocks inside me, their hot seed, Nial's shoulders all I could feel. The scent of our carnal acts all I could smell.

Slowly, I opened my eyes and saw Nial's cocky smile,

then lower, the red color of his collar. I lifted my hand to mine and knew mine was just as red.

"I want to stay right here," Ander murmured, kissing my neck. "Buried balls deep in your ass."

My pussy clenched with pleasure and Ander chuckled.

"Through the mating bond, I know you want that, too. You naughty, horny little girl."

I angled my head back so I could look at Ander. He was pleased and relaxed... sated.

"You want to stay buried in my ass, mate?" I tightened my inner muscles and he hissed.

"Gods, yes. But since it would be extremely difficult to walk buried inside you, perhaps we can part long enough to take you somewhere private."

"The Prime's chambers. Our chambers," Nial said.

Ander carefully slipped from me before Nial lifted me up and off his lap. On shaky legs, I stood beside Ander as the crowd cheered. Nial raised his hand and silence fell at once, all eyes on him.

"I am Nial Deston, your Prime. This is my second, Ander, and our mate, Lady Jessica."

The crowd rose to their feet and spoke in unison. "May the gods witness and protect you."

The spoken blessing sent a shiver down my spine as every pair of eyes I met in the crowd was dark and so very serious. I lifted my hand to my throat, eager to see for myself that our collars were now all a matching shade of red. My mates' seed slipped down my thighs but I stood tall. A queen. I knew I wouldn't have felt so powerful, so invincible without my mates at my side. I *felt* them. Their happiness, their satisfaction, their love.

My eyes flared at the last and I glanced from one to the other. "You love me?"

"Yes, mate. I love you," Ander said.

"Love is a pitiful word for what I feel." Nial bowed to the crowd, acknowledging their blessing as I struggled with what to say.

"But—"

"The collar does not lie, mate, and neither do we," Nial said.

I felt the truth of his words, saw it in his eyes, felt it in his hand that held mine, in the bond between us, newly formed.

Ander picked me up as if I weighed nothing and carried me out of the arena as Nial fell into step beside us. The old me, the Earth me, knew I should be embarrassed that everyone on the planet had just watched me have sex with my mates, but the new me, the strong woman surrounded my two warriors who loved her? She didn't give a damn.

Let them watch. Let them all see how hot and sexy and big my mates were. Let them hear my screams and envy my pleasure.

I laid my head on Ander's chest and let my love flow to them through my collar. Tomorrow I would worry about what it meant to be a queen. I would explore my new world and learn how I could serve and honor this proud warrior people. Right now, I was just going to drown in happiness. I had never been this content, this joyful, in my entire life. "Thank you."

Nial looked at me from where he walked beside us, but it was Ander who spoke. "For what? If it's for fucking you, believe me, it was our pleasure."

I smiled as tears gathered in my eyes. I'd almost missed this. My life would have been something entirely different without them. "For coming to Earth. For saving me. For taking me with you and for being mine."

"We are yours, Jessica. And we're going to prove it to you for the rest of the day." Nial reached over to wipe the tear from my cheek.

"Again... and again... and again." Ander would have kept going, but I pressed my fingers to his lips to silence him. I could just imagine what my men had in mind, but I could only feel the delicious need to surrender, to be whatever they needed me to be. There was only one thing for me to say.

"Yes."

The cheers and applause of the Prillon people faded as I was carried off by my two mates, eager to begin our new life together.

THE END

STORMY NIGHT PUBLICATIONS WOULD LIKE TO THANK YOU FOR YOUR INTEREST IN OUR BOOKS.

If you liked this book (or even if you didn't), we would really appreciate you leaving a review on the site where you purchased it. Reviews provide useful feedback for us and for our authors, and this feedback (both positive comments and constructive criticism) allows us to work even harder to make sure we provide the content our customers want to read.

If you would like to check out more books from Stormy Night Publications, if you want to learn more about our company, or if you would like to join our mailing list, please visit our website at:

www.stormynightpublications.com

21653597R00098

Printed in Poland
by Amazon Fulfillment
Poland Sp. z o.o., Wrocław